MW00990317

Cookies and Haunted Screams

A Yummy Bites Cozy Mystery

Ava Zuma

CleanTales Publishing

Other books in the Yummy Bites Series

A Yummy Bites Cozy Mystery

Book One

1

It was dark and the chilly morning breeze drew with it the scent of wild flowers from the nearby farms as Jessica Nomvete walked down the town's main street. It was 5a.m., the earliest she had ever reported to work.

The streetlights cast a shadow of her gigantic frame on the locked shop doors as she walked past. Fort Bay was a sleepy town for most of the year, unless the cultural week was on. During that time, shops would even open for twenty-four hours across the five-day event.

There were very few people on the street. Jessica, or Jess as many called her, liked the silence of the morning. It energised her and made her believe anything was possible. It was the best mind-set to have when running a business in a small town. Sometimes, the slow days can make you want to quit.

The only thing with an early morning was her 56-year-old body didn't like the cold. If she hadn't wrapped herself in a shawl and heavy woollen coat, she'd have felt the pain in her bones.

She slowed down as she closed in on *Yummy Bites*, her bakery shop. Whenever you passed outside the shop, you caught a whiff of the baked goods inside, and this morning was no different. It was free marketing, for the scent immediately told your brain that 'you need something to eat.'

The shop had a large glass window which was covered by shutters. A bunch of keys jangled as Jess unlocked the door.

Inside, the scent was even stronger. She turned on the lights and locked the door behind her. The layout of the place was simple, with a counter, some tall stools next to a snack table, and a long couch for waiting customers. The walls were yellow and white.

Behind the counter is where all the magic happened. Two large ovens were placed a few metres from each other.

It was warmer inside, and Jess took off her shawl and jacket, revealing her thick, brawny arms. She was naturally large on nearly all fronts: she was six feet tall, with a gigantic frame, a booming voice when needed, and one of the fullest laughs you'll ever hear. She also had a knack for helping people, even when it didn't suit her. It got her in trouble a few times and she tried to cut down, but that didn't last long.

She switched on the music player and the small speakers suspended near the ceiling belted out the upbeat tunes of South African *kwaito* music. They filled the bakery with the positive energy she wanted. Besides, she was about to do something momentous.

She went about setting up her workstation behind the counter. She lined up the 6, 8, 10 and 12 inch pre-cut cardboard circles, cake levels, ruler, and offset spatula, which were more than she often used for a cake. But this wasn't an ordinary cake.

4

Jess was on a mission to assemble a 4-tier cake, the tallest she had ever made. It was for a client's wedding, and she couldn't let her down. She had already baked the four cakes the previous night, leaving some minutes to midnight. She had been too excited to get much rest, hence her early start this morning. Her mind wanted to see it come to life.

She checked on her cakes, and was relieved to find they were still intact, although she'd only been away from them for a couple of hours. One was a chocolate-peanut butter cake with cream cheese and the other was a vanilla-buttermilk cake with raspberries. It had given her short nights all week as she mulled over how she would get it done.

She started setting each one on the cardboard cake circles to keep them stable when they'd be stacked on top of each other.

Two hours later, with Jess absorbed in setting the op-tier cake on its cake circle board, there was a knock on the bakery's front door.

When she opened, a shorter woman of similar age walked in wearing a fur coat on top of her shiny blue dress and heels. Lerato Ndaba, her long-time friend and business partner, was carrying a handbag and a large shopping bag with her. She belonged on a fashion street rather than a bakery shop, Jess mused. She locked the door again after Lerato was inside, keeping the closed sign showing. They opened at 9 a.m., and she needed that time to assemble the cake.

Lerato's eyes widened. "*Anti*! What on earth is going on here?"

"What do you mean?" Jess asked.

5

Lerato walked around the four cakes set atop the worktable in all their splendour. "Are these going to be two cakes?"

"These are for one," Jess replied. She hadn't told Lerato what she was baking for the wedding, working alone on the project. When she had nerves about something, she some-times went for it alone. It was a strength and weakness. She could take risks fast without slowing down for the opinions of others, but when things got complex, she rarely asked for help.

Lerato's jaw dropped as she shook her head in disbelief.

Jess frowned. "Why do you think I asked you to come with the dowels? I sure hope you didn't leave them at home."

Lerato reached into the large shopping bag and took out two packers of wood dowels, handing them to Jess. "Of course, I came with them. But wait. You remember how hard it was for you to create just two-tier cakes the first time?"

"But how many of those have we made since then? We've become the queens of that in the town. Today, we'll try something new."

"You're really serious about this, huh?"

Jess gave her trademark warm smile. "Lerato, when have I ever not followed through on something I had in mind?"

Lerato chuckled. "We've been friends for ages! You're sure you want me to dig up the archives? You might not like what you find."

"Do your worst," Jess said as she waved her off and opened the dowel packs. She set them next to the ruler.

"Even if I did, you know I'll do it with love. Need some help with the dowels?"

"Of course, I do. I've just finished setting the top cake on its board base. These dowels are what I needed the most. Now we can get started on the stacking. There's no way this cake is going to fall apart during the bride's reception."

"Why do you always make the crazy cakes no one else does?" Lerato asked.

"I was thinking about it today then I remembered why. It's probably because of Dad. He used to be a carpenter and always made unusual furniture."

"Didn't you want to make one for practice first? I mean, four tiers is pretty high," Lerato said. "Why jump from two to four?"

"Because we're dreamers. Quit with the worrying. Help me measure these dowels."

Jess measured each cake's height and cut dowels suited for the thickness. The dowels acted as columns to support each cake's base and prevent them from falling. Once marked, Lerato cut each dowel to the required length.

When Lerato was done, Jess tasked her with something else. The clock was ticking.

"Those look good. Quick, make for me some more butter cream," Jess said.

Lerato raised a brow. "You're keen to have me ruin my outfit before anyone sees it, right?"

"You work at a bakery, Lerato. Who are you trying to impress with an apron covering your clothes? Your husband isn't here."

"Leave my husband out of this. I can look good without him, right?" Lerato said. "Besides, I'm the only one who attempts to look good around here. Saving the brand's image single-handedly."

They laughed.

This is what Jess liked about her business partner, Lerato. They were friends who could laugh at each other and keep each other in check. While Jess was more spontaneous, Lerato was often level headed and cautious in her approach to things. They clashed sometimes, but their relationship had stood the test of time.

The third member of the *Yummy Bites* team arrived at 8.30 a.m., thirty minutes from the expected staff arrival time. Penny Mtanse, her long natural hair tied in a ponytail, hurried into the bakery wearing a long jacket. She was taking short, quick breaths.

Jess gave her the once over. "Was someone chasing you?"

Penny shook her head, delaying her response by about a minute as she caught her breath.

"I knew I was running late, and your voice kept ringing in my ears."

"Oh come on Penny," Jess said. "It's not like I'm running a boot camp here. You're in your late thirties. The only running you should do is on a treadmill, not to work."

"Then you better stop talking like a drill sergeant," Lerato said with a cheeky wink.

"Now you're just making things up," Jess said. "You don't have to sweat it, Penny. I mean, it's been obvious keeping time has been tricky for you the last couple of weeks. Just text me, I'll understand."

"Have you forgotten I was on time yesterday?" Penny asked. "It's not a thing, you know."

"I was speaking generally," Jess said.

Penny shrugged. "I was going to be on time today as well, but the craziest thing happened. I was driving down the country road past old Gerald's farms when out of nowhere, a squirrel jumped on the road and stopped right in front of me!"

"Oh? Don't tell me you hit it," Jess said.

"That's the thing I was going to do. I had a tractor coming up the other side of the road, and you know how narrow it is. I was stuck, and my old jalopy's brakes aren't the best in the world. So it was either the squirrel jumps out, I jump out or I hit it," Penny said.

"And then what happened?" Lerato asked.

"I swerved to the left and went off the road. I came to a stop right next to the creature. We looked at each other's eyes and then it scurried off into the bushes," Penny said.

Jess shook her head. "You have the craziest encounters. Who locks eyes with a squirrel? Did your car get damaged?"

"No, I stopped short of Old Gerald's fence. I know he'd have kicked a fuss if I went through it," Penny replied. Suddenly, she froze. She had spotted the four-tier cake, which was already assembled. "Oh, wow."

Jess beamed. She enjoyed pushing the limits and having people wonder how she did it.

"How does it look? We're going to add some buttercream to it."

Penny moved closer to the cake, circling it. "This is mind-blowing. Wow."

Jess turned to Lerato. "You see? That's how you should appreciate new levels."

"But I did," Lerato protested.

Jess corrected. "You were more sceptical than celebratory."

"Why didn't you guys tell me you were working on this yesterday?" Penny asked.

"Well, that would've ruined the surprise, right?" Jess said. She knew Penny loved trying new recipes. She was eager to learn after quitting her desk job to pursue her fresh interest: baking. Besides, Jess just wanted as few distractions as possible, and Penny was full of stories that could've derailed her.

"Okay, enough of the ogling. Lerato, let's finish coating it with butter cream. It should go out before ten," Jess said, clapping her hands in motivation.

"On it," Lerato said as she went for the tube of buttercream. Penny stopped back to watch the two women work.

The ecstatic maid of honour collected the cake, and Jess left the bakery to ensure it was in good hands during the wedding.

Jess was enjoying the sight of guests enjoying the cake at the wedding reception when her phone rang. It was Lerato. "Jess, can you talk?"

"Yeah, sure," Jess said.

"You need to come down here right now if you can," Lerato said.

Jess clutched her necklace. "What's going on?"

"It's bad news. But you have to see it for yourself," Lerato said in a grave voice.

2

As Jess closed in on the bakery, she found the road filled with traffic. This was unusual, and after twenty minutes of not moving, she parked on a side street. She hurried to the bakery.

As she got closer, she realised the cause of the traffic was right outside her bakery. There was a fire truck parked outside it. What was a *fire truck* doing there?

"Oh no," she muttered as her heart raced. Jess started running. She saw a small crowd gathered outside the bakery, but her eyes kept studying the building's roof and walls. She could see a small cloud of smoke filtering out of the front door, but no flames. Where was the smoke coming from? And why were people standing so close to the building?

"Jess!" Lerato said as she saw her partner arrive. "Thank God you're here."

"What's going on?" Jess asked as she walked to the door.

A fireman standing at the door stepped forward. "Stand back, lady."

"It's my bakery shop! Just let me see how bad it is," Jess said.

"It's not bad," Lerato said, pulling her away from the door. "It was just a scare."

Jess turned to her. "What do you mean by scare?"

"Come, let's talk here. Penny wants to see you," Lerato replied.

Standing at the edge of the small crowd was a contrite Penny. Her hair was falling on her shoulders and she was shuddering as if it were freezing, although the afternoon was beautiful and sunny, perfect for weddings but not fires.

"I'm so sorry about this," Penny said.

A worried Jess drew closer to Penny. "Are you okay?"

"I'll be fine," Penny said.

"She's a little shaken by what happened. Tell her about it," Lerato said.

Penny inhaled. "It was my fault. Lerato told me your son is graduating, so I decided to make him some cookies using a recipe I've been trying out at home. Lerato left for the market to buy some almonds we need for an order. I got out to talk to a friend on the phone and I guess I took too long. Next thing I saw was smoke coming out of the door and the fire alarm went off. I panicked and rushed into the shop. I couldn't see anything and I'm so glad the firefighters got here so fast. If they weren't here, I have no idea what I would've done. I've never fought a fire before."

Jess wrapped an arm over her shoulders. "First things first, are you okay? Did you inhale any smoke?"

"I'm fine. Just coughed a lot before they got me out."

"That's great and what matters the most," Jess said, giving Penny's shoulder a gentle squeeze.

"Thankfully, the firefighters got here on time. The place is safe. Maybe one oven is damaged, but they're clearing everything right now before we can go back in," Lerato said.

"That's a relief. I've got no idea where we would've started if…" Jess began.

Lerato interjected. *"Eish*, forget about it. We'll be fine."

Jess turned to Penny. "What recipe is this?"

"I was making chocolate chip bacon cookies," Penny said.

Jess's eyes widened, glancing at Lerato, who shrugged.

"I was telling her it's the craziest recipe I've heard in a while," Lerato said.

"How on earth would that taste?" Jess asked.

"They taste like chocolate and the bacon adds a smoky taste to it, but this wasn't how I hoped to get that flavour out," Penny replied.

Jess laughed. "I'd say you went overboard in the flavouring department."

Half an hour later, the firemen had cleared the bakery after informing Jess she might need another oven and praising her for the fire alarm system. They left, easing the traffic on the street. The curious onlookers had moved on after realising there was nothing of note.

Jess, Lerato, and Penny assessed the damage inside. Other than a trail of black on top of the oven that almost reached the ceiling and the powerful smell of burnt cookies, everything was intact.

"We'll have to get a lot of incense to get that smell out," Lerato remarked.

"It will clear in a couple of days," Jess said.

Just then, the door jingled, signalling the arrival of a client. The trio turned to the door in time to see two men standing at the door, their noses sniffing the air. At the front was a bald-headed older man who wore a cream coat, black pants and shiny black shoes. The younger man behind him wore a pinstripe blue shirt tucked into a pair of jeans. They had similar features, and Jess soon determined that they were father and son.

"Is this place on fire?" the older man asked.

Jess rushed to them. "No, no. We just had a fire scare with one of our ovens, but everything is fine. How may I help you?"

The older man looked over her shoulder towards the oven, his eyes studying the stained walls.

"Seems to me you need more of my help. I can help you fix that," the man said.

"You're in the interiors business?" Jess asked.

"The name is Al Rocki. I'm in real estate. This is my son, Tau," the man replied. "I renovate places and make them liveable again. There are people who can handle these repairs. I'll give you a discount."

Jess giggled nervously. "I appreciate the offer, but we don't need a full-on renovation."

"It will just be the wall then," Al said. "No strings attached."

"You're sure there are no strings?"

"None. It's on the house. I've heard a lot about your place. You've got some cookies or your stock was affected?"

"Erm, we've got some stashed away. Which do you need?" Jess asked.

"Get me ginger cookies for twenty-five. I want to treat my men," Al said. "Five each should make it a pack of over a hundred, right?"

"A hundred and twenty-five," Jess said, her mind racing. "I may not have all those ginger cookies. Do you mind taking some cinnamon as well?"

"Sounds good to me, right, Tau?" Al said, glancing at his son. Tau nodded back without saying a word.

"Cinnamon and ginger cookies coming up," Jess said as she motioned at Lerato and Penny. She was glad that they had already worn the disposable gloves and were packing the baked goods into the custom carton packs.

To buy time, Jess made small talk. "So you're renovating something in town?"

"Yes. I bought the House of Baron some miles from here at the edge of town. Pretty run down place. Going to make it into a nice motel for travelling guests and tourists. This is a beautiful town. More people need to experience its history, and the House of Baron is a good place to start."

As he spoke, Jess's smile had disappeared. "House of Baron? Wasn't that place set to be demolished?"

"Those were rumours. Houses built fifty years ago like that one were made to last for a century at the very least. It's still in great shape," Al replied. "It should be ready in a few weeks."

"What drives you to do this?" Jess asked, casting a casual glance at her partners. They were almost done.

"I like giving things a second chance. I've always been a fan of the underdog, kind of like the story of my life."

"I'd like to hear more about it," Jess said.

"If your cookies are good, I'll invite you to the launch when the motel opens."

Just then, Lerato and Penny came with two branded bags containing four cartons of cookies. They handed them to Al.

"Nice packaging," Al said as he reached for his wallet. "How much will that be?"

"Just four hundred rand," Jess replied.

Al handed her three two-hundred-rand notes. "That's a tip to brighten your day."

Jess beamed. "Thanks. Our phone numbers are on the bags, in case you're still keen to invite us for the launch."

"Wish us luck and you'll be there," Al said. The two men left.

Jess turned to find Penny and Lerato frowning.

"What?" Jess asked.

"You should have wished him luck. He'll need it," Lerato said. "You know the things people say about that house."

Jess shrugged. "Maybe it's all talk."

"No, it's not," Penny chimed in. "My father worked for the council. They used to get cases of homeless people spending a night there and either going mad or talking about seeing strange figures there."

"We've all heard the stories about it being haunted. But you've seen Al. He doesn't look shaken one bit. Sometimes truth is better than fiction," Jess said.

"The family abandoned that house after their father died for a reason. It would've been better to have it torn down," Penny said. "Now it's only a matter of time."

"A matter of time for what?" Jess asked.

"I have a feeling that since they're renovating it, what might happen will be far worse than scary sightings," Penny warned.

3

As sunset fell outside and the streets quietened down, Jess thought about Penny's ominous words.

It wasn't a secret that the House of Baron, built and owned by wine magnate Henry Baron, had been one place to avoid while in Fort Bay. From the homeless leaving terrorised to the sighting of shadowy figures in its compound, everyone believed it was cursed and haunted. If you asked locals what curse it was, everybody pointed to the fact Henry Baron died under mysterious circumstances while living in it. Some people say he had a long illness, others said someone slowly poisoned him until he died. No one knew the truth.

Although he was buried elsewhere by his family, they considered his holiday home his favourite spot, and that his spirit had never left it. Jess didn't believe in such stuff. Although she was spiritual, she felt idle minds paraded the myth. It was just an old building that had been rundown for far too long, losing its former glory as one of the most prestigious houses in the town. Found at the edge of town, vineyards and a small stream at the bottom of a gradual incline surrounded it. It had beautiful views of the farmlands around it and the nearby Fort Hills. It had stood out like a sore thumb amid such beauty, and Jess could understand why Al bought the place. A potential tourist attraction.

Lerato and Penny continued telling stories of strange occurrences at the place for the rest of that evening until it was time to close. Penny wanted to try the cookie recipe once more with the remaining oven, but Jess declined. She needed to clear her head, and there was no bacon left, anyway. They all left for their homes at eight o'clock. Jess had moved her car from the side street back to her spot outside the bakery and was glad she didn't have to walk down the dark streets after all the chilling stories she had heard.

Jess looked forward to getting home. She was excited that her two daughters, Faith, an interior designer and Lesedi, a tour and travel consultant, were visiting to attend their brother Will's graduation. She had missed them. Faith was engaged to Amos, an architect, and she lived in her own place several blocks from Jess' house. Lesedi had moved to the nearby town of Fernblock, a farming town next to Lake Bessie that was a favourite with tourists.

She lived in a small, gated neighbourhood with three bedroomed houses. The house was too big now after her daughters left, but she couldn't move. The memories made there were too precious. When she arrived home, Jess could hear the animated chatter from the car park. The catch up session was in full swing. When she opened the door and walked in, there was a collective cheer as the two women rushed to hug her.

"If you visited more often, you wouldn't need to be so dramatic," Jess said.

"Cut us some slack, Mum. We're here now," Faith said.

"You've fed them, Will?" Jess asked.

Will pointed at empty boxes of fast food. "I bought them some take out."

"You couldn't cook for your sisters?" Jess asked.

Will shook his head. "I'm not going to kill myself in the kitchen yet. I've got a big day tomorrow. Actually, on that note, allow me to go up and prep."

With that, Will went up the stairs.

"Your kid brother is spoiled," Jess remarked.

"Raising us well isn't spoiling us," Lesedi said.

They chatted late into the night. When she eventually turned in, Jess had one of the most restful nights she'd had in recent memory.

The next morning, they helped each other to prepare for Will's graduation. They left in Jess' minivan for Fort Bay University, one of the oldest in the county.

As the graduates were called, Faith leaned into Jess's ear.

"I wish dad was here as we added a lawyer to the family," Faith said.

Jess tensed up. She didn't like talking about *him*. "Now's not the time."

"I know we hate to talk about it, but wouldn't it be nice for him to see how far we've come?" Faith said.

"I said not now, Faith!"

"She's right, Mum," Lesedi said, backing her sister. "Maybe he thought we wouldn't make it. Well, we're doing just fine, thank you."

Jess sighed. "I once thought the same. Now, I want nothing to do with him. Let's just be grateful God has brought us this far."

The matter wasn't raised again, and Will graduated with first class honours. They went for a family brunch afterwards where they let loose with family memories, dancing and some karaoke. It was a memorable day for them all, and they went back to Jess' place as a merry bunch.

Jess' daughters went back to their lives, and weeks passed.

While having a slow afternoon at the bakery, Jess' phone rang. It was a strange number, but the voice was familiar.

"You gave me some of the tastiest cookies I've eaten in a long time. My people wanted more, but I didn't want them to get used to it," Al Rocki said with a chuckle.

Jess smiled. "Thank you for the kind words. I'll tell my team that your people loved them."

"They deserve to hear that. As another way of saying thank you, I wanted to hire you to supply some of those cookies and other foodstuffs at the launch of the motel. Consider this my official invitation."

"Thank you very much. What kind of things do you want?" Jess asked as she took a notebook and scribbled his requests. "All that is doable. When is the launch?"

"Tomorrow afternoon. You can come at around noon."

Jess almost said no. It was short notice. "You expect a hundred people?"

"Yes. Is that a problem?" Al asked.

It was a problem because she believed more time would be ideal, but for some reason, Jess couldn't turn him down. "We'll figure it out. At the end of the day, just know that we'll be there."

"I like the sound of that. See you tomorrow," Al replied and hung up.

Jess turned to Penny and Lerato. Lerato was prepping some dough while Penny sat in the corner, reading a recipe book. "Guys, we've got a big job for tomorrow afternoon. It's all hands on deck and you might go home a little late."

Lerato sat up, excited. "Well, I'm ready for some work. What's the gig?"

"Al Rocki is launching his motel tomorrow afternoon," Jess said.

Lerato's smile disappeared. "Oh no, count me out."

"We're going to be professionals instead of fear mongers," Jess said. "Lerato, you'll handle the cookies and tarts. Penny, you'll handle the hotdogs and I'll handle the small cakes and buns. Let's get to work."

"Alright," Lerato said reluctantly.

Jess had heard no reaction from Penny. She walked over to where she sat. "Are we on, Penny?"

Nothing.

Jess nudged Penny gently. Startled, Penny jumped from her seat and spun round in a panic.

"What? What?" she said, as if she was being hunted down.

Jess frowned. "Wow, you were asleep?"

Penny came to her senses and rubbed her eyes. "Sorry, I think I dozed off."

"That's the third time this week. You've also been coming early and leaving really late. Are you sleeping at home?" Jess asked.

Penny kept rubbing her eyes. "Just a little here and there."

"How come?" Jess prodded.

"Things haven't been great between Lawrence and me," Penny said.

Lerato eased up to Penny. "What do you mean?"

"We've just been arguing about stuff. I can't explain it much, but it's been bad. We can't have a simple conversation. I don't even know how we got here."

"And you stay away from the house to avoid talking to him?" Jess asked.

"Better to arrive when he's asleep and leave before he wakes up," Penny said.

Jess sighed. "I'm so sorry to hear that. I don't know what to say. But this too shall pass. Just take it a day at a time."

"I'm not so sure about that because I don't know how long it will take to get out of this," Penny said.

Jess was at a loss. Since her husband had left years ago, she'd learned to live on her own while raising her children. Most of the memories of her husband were foggy. She knew she wasn't best placed to offer Penny advice. She pursed her lips and looked at Lerato for help.

"Come here, darling. Let's go for a short walk," Lerato said as she reached for Penny's hand. They walked out into the sunny street. Jess stood looking out of the store window, silently praying that she could get them both together in time for the launch the next day.

It felt like facing their fears was something they needed, and the House of Baron was the perfect excuse. She just hoped they would find good fortune there instead of the bad luck everyone kept talking about.

4

It was the day of the launch, and Jess could tell Lerato and Penny were jittery. They had been whispering nervously between themselves all morning ever since they arrived at the bakery.

As they packed the boxes of their baked goods into the back of Jess' minivan, Lerato and Penny finally spoke up.

"Do we have to do this ourselves? Can't we hire some ushers to stand in for us?" Lerato asked.

"I was wondering the same thing. Jess, I've got a friend who runs an ushering service company and they are more than willing to take this off our hands," Penny said.

Jess shook her head. "Are you two still living in the rumour mill? How come we have heard nothing weird happening there? In case you forgot, it's launch day! It wouldn't be happening if something bad had happened."

"Maybe it's going to happen today. To make a spectacle. These spirits are pretty smart too," Penny said.

Jess chuckled. "Now you're just cracking me up."

Lerato grunted. "You won't be laughing when the inevitable happens."

"Guys, it's just a job. A pretty well paying one, too. No need to give it to another company when we can do it ourselves. Nothing will happen to us, I promise," Jess said.

"You always tell us how you're a good listener. How come you're not listening to us now?" Penny asked.

"Penny, you're usually the one who tells us to speak life and be positive about things. How about practising what you preach now?" Jess countered.

"This is hitting a lot closer to home," Penny said.

Jess sighed and adopted her commanding voice. "This is pure fiction that has gained a life of its own. I need you two to be on top of your game. I get a feeling we could have a long working relationship with these guys. So let go of the rumour mill, let's do our jobs. Okay?"

Penny straightened. "When you put it that way, we're going to make it happen."

"That's more like it. Lerato, are we on the same page?"

Lerato sighed. "I'd never leave you in a fix. Let's do this."

When they arrived at the location where the House of Baron was supposed to be, an impressive repainted building met them with the same facade but an air of freshness that was inviting.

Now renamed as *Dreams Motel,* the large twenty-room mansion had received a new lease of life. Not only was the paint done, but all the cracks on its stone walls were fixed up or strengthened. They had replaced the rotting window frames with freshly treated wood. The overgrown grass outside was all trimmed down and the whole compound landscaped, keeping some of the old designs and adding some new seedlings and a fountain. It looked like a great place to be, Jess thought.

The paved driveway replaced the dirt one from the past, and an array of high end cars stood outside as Jess parked her minivan next to one of them.

"I have to say I'm impressed with this," Penny said.

"So your fears are gone?" Jess said.

"Fears? What fears?"

They all laughed.

Tau came to receive them. He wore a pristine white shirt and white pants that looked like they were being worn for the first time.

"Welcome to Dreams Motel," he said with a smile. "Follow me."

He led them to the banquet hall, which was decked out in white and gold ribbons. The theme was rebirth, and white was a fitting choice in Jess' eyes. There were standing tables with a candle stand and a vase with a few roses placed across the room, and a podium at the front of the room with a microphone stand. An enormous banner hung over the front of the room that read 'New beginnings start here. Dreams Motel.' There were some house music playing softly in the background. A few early guests in tuxedos stood talking to each other, glasses in hand.

Al walked up to Jess and her team, hands held out wide, with a satisfied grin. He, too, was dressed in an all-white suit and shoes. "Wonderful! You made it on time."

"An hour before the event, just as you asked," Jess said.

"I'm loving your service already," Al said. "Tau will show you to the table we set for you. I'm expecting around a hundred people here."

Jess gave the room a casual scan. "We can handle that and a little more."

"Fantastic," Al said as he rubbed his hands. Jess noticed the expensive rings on both ring fingers, and the designer watch on his wrist.

After they had set up the baked goods on their table, Jess and her team changed into a simple blouse and black skirt outfit with a colourful scarf branded in the bakery's house colours.

"We're not just here to make some cash. We're selling ourselves," Jess said.

An hour later, the place was nearly full, the music louder, the chatter more animated and the atmosphere jolly.

While Lerato manned the table, Jess and Penny walked amongst the guests every ten minutes with trays full of baked goodies. Judging by the smiles, the enthusiastic chewing and the calls for more, the guests were loving what they had made.

She expected Al to make a speech, but all he did was give opening remarks that were short and informal.

"We're not here for a corporate event. This is a holiday house meant to sell relaxation and enjoyment. We're here to give you a taste instead of boring you with speeches. So take a bite, a drink, mingle and enjoy yourselves! Everything is on the house," Al said when he stood on the podium. After that, the mood in the place lightened up.

As she went about her rounds, Jess started feeling her phone vibrating in her waist pouch. She ignored it the first two times, but on the third time she had to stop and check. It was Will calling. Jess stepped out of the banquet hall into the quieter corridor. "Is everything okay at home?"

"Mum, I went out to meet some friends and I've somehow misplaced the house key. Is there one you've stashed somewhere?" Will asked.

"I don't do those kinds of things. If you need the key, you'll have to come and get it from me."

"Argh," Will said. "You're pretty far, right? I just needed to get something from the house and head out again."

"Well, for starters, you should never make that sound to me again. Second, I'm right on the edge of town, where the House of Baron was."

"The haunted house?"

Jess corrected. "It's not haunted. They've renovated it into a motel."

"Wait, are you serious?" an excited Will said. "Maybe I could come by."

"What time?" Jess asked, but Will had already hung up. She shook her head and went back inside. When she walked back to the table, it surprised her to see only a few items left.

"We're almost out and everyone is raving about them. What if we have a riot after such success?" Lerato said with a smile.

"Look at you, having a good time," Jess teased.

"Well, a lot of things have surprised me today," Lerato replied. "I'm open to a little fun, too."

Jess went for one more round, and her tray lasted five minutes. As she walked back to the table, she knew she might find no refills. She was a few steps from it when she heard a shriek. It came from the right part of the room, but the music partly masked how loud it was. But Jess had an ear for sounds, and she turned to see where it came from. Then the shriek grew louder until the deejay lowered the music. The anguished sound filled the room.

"Wake up, please wake up!" a woman said.

Jess used her enormous frame to make way in between the guests. With her height, she could see what looked like an open office door. When she got there, she saw Al slumped in his leather chair, unmoving. A woman lay her head on his chest, sobbing while tugging at his coat.

"Why are you leaving me?" she wailed.

Even from where she stood, Jess could see the colour had drained from Al's face. He wasn't coming back. The man was dead.

5

Jess froze where she was, watching events before her unfold as if in slow motion.

Someone grabbed the wailing woman from Al's chest and pulled her away. The woman's elaborate makeup was now a messy blotch on her face, and Jess could hardly tell who it was. For a moment, Al lay in his chair, and the sight saddened Jess. The man of influence reduced to a shell. It gave her a wave of guilt and awareness of her own mortality. Two men who rushed to Al's side blocked her view. One of them unbuttoned his shirt to the navel, revealing a white vest. The other propped up his shoulders, waiting for his partner.

They both lowered Al to the floor and started performing CPR. Jess watched the men work, one counting the compressions and prompting for the breaths to be done while the other actually performed the procedure. They worked like a machine, and for a moment Jess had hope. She rued the many times she'd postponed going for her first aid refresher courses. She'd even set a reminder after the bakery fire scare that went unheeded.

"Oh my word, this is terrible," Lerato said. Jess turned to find her partner beside her. "What happened?"

"Seems like he collapsed," Jess replied.

"Is he going to make it?"

"If anyone is worthy of being used for a miracle, it's those two men," Jess replied.

However, ten minutes later, it became clear that it was all in vain. By that time, the paramedics had arrived to boost the revival efforts, but Al remained unresponsive. Jess watched them pronounce him dead at 6.24p.m.

Shocked whispers fill the room. Some people sobbed. A celebration had just turned into a grieving party.

"Oh, poor guy. What a way to go, after all that hard work," Lerato said. "He was a good man. Why is life so cruel?"

"He came across well. I feel for his family, especially his son." Jess said as she scanned the room for any sign of Tau. She saw him standing by the doorway of the office, embracing the woman who had been sobbing on Al's chest. His white shirt was now covered in stains from the woman's makeup, a dramatic display of their brokenness. Jess concluded that was his mother, and she felt the weight of their sadness.

"There he is, consoling his mum," Lerato said, putting a palm to her cheek. "This is terrible."

"Someone once said life is a series of problems. Your mission is to keep finding solutions until you leave," Jess said.

"Do you think his time had come?" Lerato asked.

"I'm not a *sangoma*," Jess said.

Lerato whispered to her. "You don't have to be a traditional healer to know this is the curse at work."

Jess shot her a look. "You're still talking about that after the magnificent work this man has done in this place?"

"You can change the look, but the inside is still the same," Lerato said. "The myths are true."

"No. I'm not buying it. No one dies without a logical reason."

"Don't look for complicated answers when the simple ones are true."

"*Yhoo*, enough with that! Don't let someone hear what you're saying. Did you cover the stand?" Jess asked, keen to derail the conversation.

"Oh, let me do that. I'll be back before you know it," Lerato said as she slipped away.

Jess didn't want her to return soon. She was keenly studying the scene before with the desire of reflecting about it after-wards. She moved closer to the door, so that she could get a better view of Al, getting there as the paramedics debated covering him before the detectives arrived. Her height advantage gave her a great bird's-eye view of her client, and another wave of sadness struck her.

Al was lifeless, his mouth agape and eyes closed. There were no marks on his body. She couldn't help the surreal compar-ison of the vibrant man she'd met hours earlier and the immobile body she saw now. In the blink of an eye, every-thing had changed. It looked natural, and Jess suspected he had a health condition. That's the only thing that made sense.

She didn't have time to keep deducing. The police arrived and took over the entire space. They herded all the guests to one side of the room, while they cordoned the office with yellow crime scene tape.

A medium-built detective with a moustache, whom other officers called Detective Meyer, led the charge. He coordinated the forensics team to collect samples and take photos of Al's body, as well as search for fingerprints. He then spoke to the two first responders about the man's condition when they found him and what they did. All this Jess observed from a distance, fascinated by how things were unfolding. She'd never been this close to a potential crime scene, although she had visited a few many years ago when she interned at a law firm.

But why would she call it a crime scene, yet they had declared nothing as foul play? Perhaps it was because of the yellow tape. Half an hour after they arrived, three detectives went around talking to guests about what they saw. One by one, people gave their responses as each detective scribbled in little notebooks.

One detective, an athletic-bodied woman in her late thirties with dark hair tied into a ponytail and wearing a trouser suit, walked up to Jess.

"Hello, I'm Detective Shelly. I'd like to ask you a few questions about what just happened. This is important for our investigation. Once we're done, you can leave," the detective said.

"Sure, I'll help in whichever way I can."

"Great. Where were you when the emergency began?"

"First, I'd like to say the deceased hired me, so this is a sad day for me as well. I was serving guests some baked treats when I heard a scream coming from the office. I walked towards it and saw a woman crying next to him. Then someone took her aside and the two men started performing CPR, but he was gone."

"Did you interact with the deceased before the incident?"

"Yes, he welcomed us alongside his son when we arrived. We chatted about a few things, and then we crossed paths maybe once twice more during the event," Jess said.

"How did he seem to you?" Detective Shelly asked.

"He seemed happy. Satisfied. Very proud. He was really looking forward to completing the transformation of this place. For so long it's had a terrible reputation."

"Everyone around town knows those stories. So you didn't notice if he looked unusual or if there was anything around him that was out of place?"

Jess paused for a moment to scrub through her memory. She shook her head. "Nothing comes to mind."

The detective scribbled something in her notebook.

"What treats were you serving?" the detective asked.

"Doughnuts, cookies, tarts, some hotdogs, and buns."

"Can I have some of them?" Detective Shelly asked.

Jess pursed her lips. "We had almost run out of everything when the incident happened. I doubt there's anything left," Jess said.

"Let's check," the detective said, lifting the tape that separated them.

Jess went under the tape and walked to her table stand. It had been arranged by Lerato earlier, so everything looked neat. To her surprise, she found two plates covered in foil with snacks. One contained five doughnuts and the other seven cookies.

"I'll have to take both plates with me," Detective Shelly said as she took the plates.

Jess extended her arm to block her. "Hold on. Why? Do you think he was murdered?"

"No, I think the man may have died a natural death. Whether that's true, I leave in the hands of the pathologist. I'd like to see if your bites were a contributing factor."

"I keep my ingredients natural, so there's nothing you'll find," Jess said.

"I'm sure you use your best ingredients. But for some people, wheat and sugar can be a matter of life and death," Detective Shelly said.

Jess saw the sense in it and allowed her to take the two plates. They wrapped the treats in clear film and were unlikely to fall over.

"Is that all?" Jess asked.

"Yes, this will be all for now. Thank you for your time," Detective Shelly said.

Jess hung back as they questioned Lerato as well, although hers was much shorter.

By the time the guests had all given testimony, the scene processed, and the body taken downtown, there was an air of uncertainty. People lingered on after the police left, and then they started leaving for their homes, one at a time. No one had been arrested and to most, it seemed like a natural death.

"Let's head out. The longer we stay here, the more it rubs off on us," Lerato said as she took the last of their utensils and placed them in a carton box.

"What rubs off on us?" Jess asked.

"The curse."

"I thought you said the bad things only happen when you're inside the motel. Why would they follow us home?"

Lerato shrugged. "Never joke with the spirit world. What you can't see can surprise you."

Jess almost laughed in mild amusement. "I could say the same to you. Don't believe in it until you let your imagination run away from reason."

"It's wise that you're holding that laugh! You might anger it!"

"You're right, it's not time to laugh. But you're being outrageous," Jess replied. She had to endure more of Lerato's perspectives about the House of Baron and how making it into the Dreams Motel without appeasing its restless ghost was a mistake. Jess dropped her off and headed home. She felt the exhaustion of the day's events creep up on her.

As she parked her car in the car park outside, she expected to find Will seated outside, sulking. He didn't come for the house key. Instead, she saw the living room lights peeking through the drawn curtain. When she got into the house, she found him seated in front of the wide-screen TV, watching a movie. He'd propped himself up on the couch with his legs propped on the ottoman, with a pack of potato crisps next to him. He didn't even turn to see her come in.

"Hey, Mum," Will muttered.

"How do you know it's me and you didn't even turn to look?" Jess asked.

"I just know."

"You didn't come for the key."

"Ah, I found it had slipped into my inner jacket pockets."

"Keys don't slip into those inner pockets. You put it there and forgot," Jess said.

"I guess," Will replied.

"What have you made for dinner?" Jess asked, already knowing the answer.

Will shrugged and lifted the bag of crisps. "That's it for me."

Jess shook her head and sighed. Her two daughters scoured through job adverts after their graduations, eager to escape the nest. Will was showing signs of the opposite, and she didn't want to let it fester. She wanted to give him a piece of her mind, but was too tired to see it through. She'd just make a burger and call it a night.

As she did this, her mind raced back to the event. The police had taken the few treats she had left. Could they have triggered Al's condition? She suddenly gave up on the burger idea and settled for an apple instead.

She wasn't sure how she'd live with the news that one of her baked goodies had caused someone's untimely death during a memorable time in their lives. The thought of Yummy Bites becoming death bites made her shudder.

6

The next morning, the persistent chirping of a bird outside her bedroom window stirred Jess awake. She rubbed her eyes and glanced at her clock. It was 6.30a.m, a little later than her usual waking hour of 5a.m. But she was still early and took her time to get out of bed. She walked to the window, pulling back the curtain slowly, and saw the black and crimson-coloured bird standing on the sill. Perhaps it was calling to its mates, which were common in the area. She smiled, and it caught the bird's attention. It gave her the side eye, chirped one more time and then took off.

She lingered at the window, watching other birds flutter by, admiring the gentle sway of the trees. Behind the clump of trees were fields of grapes that supplied both fresh fruit and wine to the town. It was a refreshing morning, and she felt energised for the day.

Jess went down the stairs. The house was dead quiet, and in the living room she found the now empty bag of crisps on the couch. Will was not present as he was sleeping in again.

With a sigh, Jess picked up the bag and trashed it, and spruced up the room.

She took a shower and left for the bakery without seeing Will. She made a mental note to have a chat with him when she got back that evening.

There's never much traffic in the small town unless it was the cultural parade season. During those days, she'd still go to work while most people took the time off to put on fancy costumes and dance in the streets. Jess arrived at the bakery shop at 7.30 a.m. thinking she'd be the first to arrive. Lerato often slept in the day after an event, and Jess didn't expect her to arrive until 9 a.m. But it surprised her to find Penny already at the shop, working.

"This is new," Jess said as she closed the door behind her.

Penny smiled as she put on her apron. "It's good to try something new at times. How's your morning?"

"Oh, it's fantastic. How's yours?"

"It's just getting started. I've got some news for you, but I also want to hear some news from you," Penny said.

Jess raised a brow. "News from me? About what?"

"There's something that happened last night, I'm told," Penny said with a wink.

"Why do rumours travel so fast in this place? Who told you?"

"A neighbour of mine heard it from someone else and called me last night," Penny said. "But before you give me the juicy details, I was wondering if you'd help me make a tiered strawberry fruit cake."

Jess frowned. "*Eish*, you know that's a difficult one, even for me. Why not choose something simpler?"

"You're the one who says it's good to try new things," Penny said.

"But it doesn't mean you take shortcuts. It took me years to be able to say that. Take it a day at a time," Jess advised.

"Fair enough. So, what happened yesterday?"

"What have you heard?"

"That someone collapsed at the House of Baron."

"Dreams Motel, that's what it's called now. And trust me, it wasn't juicy. It was really sad to see," Jess said.

Penny tilted her head to her right side. "Well, tell me more."

The door jingled, and Lerato came in.

"Good morning, ladies," Lerato bellowed.

"You're both surprising me today. Lerato, we're used to you sleeping in after gigs," Jess teased.

"Heh! After yesterday's events, I couldn't sleep properly," Lerato said.

"I've been waiting for hours for you to tell me about it," Penny said.

Lerato stopped, her eyes widening. "You know about it already?"

"At this rate, everyone in town has their version of what happened," Jess said.

"Tell me about it then! You had a front-row seat," Penny urged.

Jess sighed. "First, don't make it sound so dramatic. This isn't entertainment. I'm still shaken by what happened, as I've never had a client die on me before. Anyway, the place is all renovated and looks nothing like how it was. I really like all the hard work Al put in to fix up the place. The guests were great. We ran out of our bites in record time, and everything was going well. Then I heard a scream, and then we learned Al had collapsed. They tried to save him, but it was too late."

"That's so sad," a more sombre Penny said.

"Hold on, girls. I know Jess said it's not entertainment, but you've left out so many important details," Lerato said.

"Oh, there's more?" Jess asked.

"That place looks like a royal palace! Dreams Motel is so fitting because it is the palace of dreams. The decor, the seats, the rooms, the banquet hall, everything was so well put together. Al himself was such a cool guy. He and his son received us when we arrived. They gave us a serving table, all the guests just binged on our products. It was unbelievable. Then two guys tried to save his life and fought so hard for him, doing chest compressions and everything. But when they announced he was dead, I felt a sadness and creepy chill sweep across the room. It was like a presence that just came down on people. I only felt free from it when Jess and I left," Lerato narrated.

"You didn't tell me about the 'presence' last night," Jess said.

Lerato frowned. "I didn't? Well, I guess when I got home I reflected and now understand better what was happening."

Jess found Lerato's enthusiasm for the whole topic troubling. Lerato was often the more level-headed, calm and precise one of the two. But today she will share as much detail on the incident as possible. It's almost as if she'd waited for years to have her fears about the House of Baron confirmed.

Penny had placed both palms on her face by now as she listened. "*Bathong*, that's crazy. On the day he was opening up the palace, too."

"I had the same thought. That's why it's so tragic," Jess added. Her phone rang. It was a number she didn't recognise.

"Yummy Bites, hello," Jess said.

A female voice replied. "Hello. Is that Jess Nomvete?"

"Yes, it is. How may I help you?"

"I'm Detective Mason calling from Mesa Police. Could you find time to come to the station at 11 a.m.?"

Jess' chest tightened. "Why would you want me there?"

"I'm afraid I can't tell you the reason on the phone. Please come by at 11 and I'll tell you more."

"What if I can't make it?"

"Then unfortunately I may have to send officers to get you," Detective Mason replied.

Jess had wanted to ask another question, but it got stuck in her throat. The detective's words sent a chill down her spine. She simply muttered, "Okay, thanks."

When she hung up the call, she found Penny and Lerato looking at her curiously.

"Who was that?" Lerato asked.

"It was the police," Jess said. "They want me to go to the police station."

"What for?" Lerato asked.

"They didn't say. I have to be there at eleven."

"That sounds weird," Lerato said. "They arrested no one yesterday, right?"

"None," Jess said. "And she said if I don't turn up, then she'll send officers to get me."

Lerato shook her head. "That sounds to me like they want to arrest you. Why would they want you without calling me?"

"Maybe they'll call you. Give them a few minutes," Jess said.

But for the next hours, as they worked, Lerato didn't receive any call from the police.

"I'll be heading out shortly," Jess announced at half past ten. "Watch the shop until I get back."

Lerato took off her apron. "There's no way they are calling you in without me. We were together."

"I can handle this," Jess said.

"*We* can handle this. I'm coming with you and that's the end of the discussion," Lerato said.

"Alright then. Penny-" Jess began, but stopped as Penny took off her apron.

"I'm coming too," Penny said.

"Girls, we can't be shutting down the business every time this happens," Jess said.

"This is the first and last time that it happens. We leave together and come back together," Lerato said.

The three women locked the shop, got into Jess' car, and left for the police station.

"Jess, can you move your seat up a little?" Penny, who was seated behind the driver's seat, asked.

"Scoot over to the other side. Do you want us to have an accident here?" Lerato said.

"Oh, sorry to distract you, driver!" Penny said as she changed positions.

Other than that brief exchange, the rest of the trip was mostly in silence. As she drove, Jess couldn't help asking two troubling questions repeatedly. She'd never been in such a situation before, and she was edgy.

Did someone spike one of her baked treats with something that killed Al? If that was the case, would she taste freedom again?

7

Mesa Police Station was like a place straight out of a dystopian novel. It was in a part of town one would consider seedy. All that was there were street-side car garages, low-income homes, and a few abandoned structures. The police station itself had impounded cars lining up every inch of its fence until you got to the gate. Inside, after a long driveway past smaller outhouses, you arrived at the main station building, which seemed to be an old bungalow converted into a police station. Outside, it was painted in faded police colours, with Mesa Police emblazoned in black paint over the entrance.

Jess parked in one of the few parking spots next to the key station building. "I'll go have a chat with them."

"Stop trying to leave out the details," Lerato said. "We're in this all the way."

The three women got out of the car and walked to the reception desk. Behind it was a sole lazy eyed officer who was staring into his mobile phone.

"I'm Jessica Nomvete. I'm here to see Detective Mason," Jess told the officer.

The officer slowly walked away and bellowed "Mason!" down a hallway. Footsteps approached and the detective that interviewed Jess at the motel appeared. She smiled.

"Thank you for making the time," Detective Mason said.

"Did I have a choice?" Jess asked.

"There are always choices. It's the consequences that you need to be aware of," the detective replied. She gave Penny and Lerato the once over. "They're with you?"

"Yes, they are," Jess replied.

"Alright. Follow me," Detective Mason said.

Jess followed her down the hallway, and they stopped at an open door. Opposite the door was a bench.

"Your friends can wait here," the detective said.

Jess gave Lerato a smile and entered the room. Detective Mason closed the door behind her. It was a simple office with a wooden desk in front of a worn leather chair, and two wood and cloth chairs where guests or visitors of the state would sit. On the walls were a shelf stacked with books about police work and a metal file cabinet.

"Have a seat," the detective said as she sat in the leather chair.

Jess sat and expected the detective to talk to her immediately. Instead, Detective Mason pored through a case file, slowly turning page after page. This went on for five minutes, and Jess began fidgeting in her chair.

"What did you summon me for?"

Detective Mason looked up. "Oh, you'll know soon enough. My boss will come to talk to you shortly."

Jess stiffened as her mind raced. Her boss? Who was he and what did he want with her?

Another five minutes went past, each getting tenser.

Suddenly the door fell open and the medium-built detective with a moustache that she'd seen coordinating the crime scene at the motel walked in. In his hands he had two clear evidence bags containing the baked bites taken from the event, and a folder. Jess remembered his name: Detective Meyer.

"Thank you for waiting for me," he said as he placed the evidence bags on the desk. He turned to Jess. "Detective Roger Meyer. I'm the lead investigator in Al's death. You're Jessica Nomvete?"

"Yes, sir. But you can call me Jess."

"Great. Mason, do you mind giving me a few minutes with Jess?"

Detective Mason was already up. "No problem, sir. Take all the time you need."

She left, and Detective Meyer paced the room in silence, as if in deep thought. When he stopped, he sat in the leather chair. By this time, Jess' anxiety was hitting the roof.

"Why do you think you're here?" he asked.

"No one has told me why I'm here," Jess said, frustration in her voice.

"Well, I have good news and not so good news. Which do you want to hear first?"

Tired of what she believed were now mind games, Jess replied with the first response that came to mind. "The 'not so good'."

"Alright. Al was poisoned. It's possible the substance was contained in one of the baked goods you had, but it could've also been in something else. We can't be sure. The good side is all samples of your bites are clean and harmless. You also don't have any history of a criminal record, which also benefits you," Detective Meyer said.

"Am I a suspect?"

"A possible suspect. We clear your name and we move to the next one."

Jess felt her shoulders sink. Her worst nightmare was coming to pass.

"So, what next?" Jess asked.

"That depends on you," the detective replied. "He had hired you to supply the treats, right?"

"Yes. He came over to my shop a few weeks earlier and loved what we made. He then got in touch to supply his event."

"Did you have any disputes about this of any kind?"

Jess shook her head. "No. In fact, he's one of the best clients I've ever had. Considerate, understanding, hands-off and willing to pay full price to support the business. He even gave us half the amount before we started. I'm quite sad it ended this way."

"What do you know about Al's death?" Detective Meyer asked.

"I only know as much as anyone. He collapsed and died. I've been wondering if he had a condition or something," Jess said.

"Have you heard of a chemical called briacolite?"

Jess's forehead furrowed. "No, what on earth is that?"

The detective leaned forward. "It's not from outer space. In fact, you can buy forms of it in the pharmacy. It's usually found in commercial energy drinks. But you can also buy a lighter powder compound from pharmacies, which gym enthusiasts and body builders used to make their own energy-booster drinks. It's blended in with something else to neutralise it and used for strength. On its own, it's deadly. It's odourless and hard to detect unless you know about it. That's what killed Al."

"Where did you find it?" Jess asked.

"We spotted small traces of it inside his mouth and his digestive tract. That's why we think it's something he ate or drank," the detective replied. "It triggered a cardiac arrest, and he was gone."

Jess sighed. "So needless."

"What?" the detective asked, craning his neck.

"It was such a needless death," Jess clarified.

"Logic isn't always straightforward with a murderer."

"I'd like you to be straight with me. Am I under arrest?"

Detective Meyer leaned back and smiled. "No, you're free to go."

Jess eyed the treats. "Should I go with these?"

"No, unfortunately you can't. It's part of due diligence. I hope you don't mind."

"No biggie. I'll just get another set of plates."

Jess rose, and the detective followed. She towered over him and he wasn't shy to react.

"You're quite the presence," Detective Meyer said. "I wish you well."

Jess wasn't sure if this was a compliment and played it safe. "Thanks and have a great day, too."

When she stepped out, Penny and Lerato stood up, anxious to hear the report.

"Let's go home," Jess announced with a beaming smile. The two women embraced her and together they walked out of the station. Jess gave them a quick summary of how it went.

As they neared the car, Penny pulled Jess to the side.

"Oh, now we have secrets?" Lerato lamented.

"It's just going to be a minute," Penny said.

They stopped next to one of the few trees on the grounds.

"I'm so glad this went well there. And again, I'm sorry about the fire the other day," Penny said. "I hope you're not fed up with my recent drama."

"Hey, that's all water under the bridge. I admire your hunger to grow and try out new things. Besides, we need some younger energy around the place. Let's keep going," Jess said.

Penny sighed in relief. "That's so good to hear. Everything has been blurry sometimes for the last couple of days, so I'm just checking in."

Jess sensed a heaviness in Penny. "Is everything okay at home?"

Penny bit her lower lip for a moment. "No, it's not. I've tried to be strong about it and I just can't."

"What's going on?"

"My marriage is falling apart. I literally feel like I'm drowning each moment I'm in that house. That's why I've been doing early mornings and some late nights. I need your help. You and Lerato need to help me," Penny said, a tear rolling down her cheek.

"I'm so sorry to hear that," Jess said as she hugged Penny. "Um, I don't know what to say. I mean, we can give you advice."

Penny pulled out of the hug. "I'm not talking about advice. I need the two of you to come to my home *physically* and save my marriage. Please."

8

In her fifty-six years of living, Jess had never received such a request before. At first, she thought it was purely because of who she was in Penny's life: her boss, someone who took her in after she quit her job, a patient teacher of baking. But then it dawned on her that Penny was hanging on to hope by a thin thread.

"Physically? You mean in person?" Jess asked.

Penny nodded. "Yes, in person. I've heard all kinds of advice and I can't take it anymore. Nothing works. This is it for me."

Jess inhaled. "Look, I appreciate the fact that you've trusted me enough to share this with me. However, I don't want to get in the middle of such a sensitive situation. You know I've been a single parent for a long time. I've lost touch with what it means to live with a partner."

"It doesn't matter. Whatever you can offer will be helpful. Plus, you'll be with Lerato."

Jess glanced towards the car. Lerato was studying her finger-nails as if craving a manicure.

"Does your husband know about this? Have you spoken to Lerato?"

"My husband wants to try something different. This is what I'll propose. Both of us will bring people we trust and hash it out. I had to talk to you before I talked to Lerato. She'll follow what you say."

"I see. Let me think about it and then I'll get back to you. In the meantime, what do you need? Time off?"

Penny shook her head. "No time off. I need to keep working. Just understand it when I come early and leave late. I'm trying to hang in there."

"You have my support. If anything else comes up, don't hesitate to tell me."

Penny dried off the tear. "I will. Thanks for listening."

The two walked back to the car.

"I'm feeling a little jealous," Lerato remarked. "Why am I not part of the plan?"

"Let's go get some lunch," Jess suggested.

"That's what you two were talking about all that time? I would've suggested a spot in less time," Lerato said.

They laughed as they drove off. They later enjoyed a hearty lunch at Timo's Spot, a place where all kinds of *braai* barbecue meats could be sampled.

After she dropped off Lerato and Penny at the bakery, Jess went for a drive. She had unfinished business, and needed to talk to Tau. She'd called him under the pretext of following up on the contract payment for the event, but she truly wanted to talk to him about what happened. Although it made her look greedy, it was the simplest and most logical reason she could think of meeting him.

As she drove, her thoughts went back to her chat with Penny. It had brought back memories of her brief marriage to Otis, memories that she'd suppressed for years. Occasionally, they resurfaced when uncertain life situations came her way, and Penny's dilemma had become a trigger without warning.

Otis was supposed to be a passing cloud. He was a talented guitarist who formed his own band in his early twenties. They specialised in live shows and they were soon known all over the coast and highlands. But she didn't get attracted to him after watching him on stage. She met him at a traffic stop, where he had strummed the guitar at her from his friend's open top sedan. Jess was driving to a doctor's appointment and needed cheering up, and she ended up meeting him after for a milkshake. They met again on and off for a few months with it looking like a regular friendship.

Then one day they went for a movie and he afterwards told her he wanted to date her. She thought about it for a week before admitting she had feelings for him, so why not explore? In her journal, she'd dubbed it as the 'Week of Misdirection', because once they started dating a lot of complications came into her life. She had three children with him and moved into his one-bedroom apartment. It soon became clear to her that dating a musician who was hardly home wasn't the right way to raise a young family, and they argued whenever he was around. Money ran thin, and she had to juggle work and tending to her young ones.

It was a hot January day when she had just finished shopping and was pushing the trolley to Otis' beaten up van when she saw him with her. She was in her late teens, much younger than her and as fresh as a bun. They were getting into her car and drove off, leaving Jess frozen next to the van. She broke down and cried for close to an hour. After that, it was only a matter of time before it officially fell apart. One time, in his customary way, he kissed each child on the forehead and told them he'd be on tour for a week and return the next week-end. They never saw or heard from him again.

Jess heard stories about him moving to the city with the young woman, and it was clear she had to move on. But she closed the door to that kind of love forever. That's why Penny's request felt so awkward for her. It was an emotional battle she hadn't experienced in decades.

Jess met Tau at Chess Restaurant, a mid-range place that served great chicken curry.

She found him seated at the corner of the landing floor, a place where he could see whoever was arriving and also get privacy from prying ears. The table wasn't close to another. He had chosen wisely, although the landing floor had one flaw: it wasn't well-ventilated.

She could tell he had discovered this problem by the fact he had a nearly full jug of water next to him. A glass filled with ice cubes was also on the table. He was downing a glass of water as she got to the table. He composed himself when he saw her, dabbing a handkerchief over his brow.

"Sorry about that," Tau said, smiling.

"It's okay. The heat here is well-known," Jess said.

"Maybe we should move elsewhere," Tau suggested as his eyes scanned the room. "But the suitable spots are full."

"This spot is great for conversation," Jess said.

"Great. Order something."

"Have you eaten already?" she asked.

Tau nodded. "I had some extra spicy curry. It was the best I've ever had, but it's causing me to experience this."

"It's better to be happy and full than to be miserable and sweaty."

They both laughed. Jess opted to order fresh and chilled orange juice.

"So, you wanted to see me about the payment," Tau said. "I can-"

Jess put a hand up to stop him. "Let's not talk about that. I want to first know how you're doing."

Tau's smile faded fast, and his eyes drifted away. He bit his lower lip to fight the tears.

"It's tough," he muttered. "But we're keeping it together."

"How's your mother doing?"

"She's being strong, like always. But it's hard on her too. They had their moments of hardship but loved each other," Tau replied. "I've been having trouble sleeping."

Jess' juice arrived, chilled just right. This prompted Tau to refill his glass and take another drink of water.

"Give it time. It will blow over. Keep your mind busy during the day. Go to the gym if you can," Jess suggested. "Don't sit alone, overthinking things."

Tau nodded. "I'll try."

"Before you saw him in his office, when was the last time you saw your father?"

Tau paused before answering. "We talked about organising a monthly event. A live band of sorts. Then invite locals to come and while away their evening. We wanted the motel to be a place where people meet, not fear. Then he told me he was going to the office to get his high blood pressure meds, but he didn't return. The next thing I heard was the screaming. I still hear it sometimes, with the same high pitch."

Instinctively, Jess placed her palm over his hand to reassure him. "A day at a time, child."

"Thanks," Tau replied. "I needed that."

"Tell me something. Did your father have any enemies?"

"Why do you ask?"

"I'm sure you already know the police are looking at the possibility that it might be a natural death or caused by something or someone else."

Tau sighed. "Yes, they told us. But why are you so interested?"

"Ever since the two of you came into my shop, I could tell you were good people. The same way you get troubled at night is the same thing I experience sometimes. If I connect with someone or an event emotionally, I sometimes can't let it go until I make it right. This is one of those times," Jess said. "I want to help you find answers. If that's not possible, then at least some peace will be good, too."

Tau pursed his lips as he digested what Jess had told him.

"The only name that comes to mind is Samkelo. It's someone that my father knew when he was younger. Samkelo has been pestering my father for money for years. He often says my father conned him, but Dad told me he had paid off his debt," Tau said. He drank the rest of the water in the glass.

"Do you know how I can find this Samkelo person?"

Tau shrugged. "I don't know. He doesn't seem to have a home."

They talked some more about life and what Tau was working on. She learned he liked basketball and archery, and had won several high school awards. He was being groomed to join his father's property business, and was an apprentice for the past two years, going everywhere his father went. He had a sharp mind for business opportunities, which Jess admired.

After their conversation, Jess offered to drop Tau home. They drove to The Springs, an upmarket gated estate bordering one of the best placed private beaches. Each house in this estate was a single story maisonette, with its own beach allocation. Tau told her it was one of several homes that Al owned in the town.

When she pulled up in front of their house, she saw the woman who was wailing on Al's chest waiting for them. She looked solemn this time round, with no makeup on her face. She wore a dark blue dress and a black shawl over her head, a mark of mourning. When she saw Tau, she smiled.

"You've brought me a visitor?" the woman asked.

Tau alighted and walked up to his mother. "This is Jess. She was serving us at the launch. She was just dropping me off."

"Well, now that she's here, I might as well invite her in for a cup of tea. Would you like some tea, Jess?" the woman asked.

Ordinarily, Jess would've said no. But the fact she empathised with the family, and this was also an opportunity to ask her questions about her husband, made it impossible to pass up.

Jess switched off the car. "Sure, I'd love some tea."

9

Jess walked alongside Mary on the lush lawn at the back of the house. It was a sizable area, with three brick gazebos at various spots connected with concrete walkways.

"We can talk here with some privacy," Mary said. The gazebo had three seats with comfort cushions. "Make yourself comfortable."

Jess obliged, and she wasn't disappointed. The seats were heavenly. "How have you been coping the last few days?"

"It's thrown a lot of things into disarray, but we'll pull through," Mary said.

"I saw it devastated you when it happened."

"I couldn't believe it. I'm sure all the guests expected to enjoy the celebration with him and not mourn him. But I lost a man I've lived with for half my life. It's a pain I can't describe. I still feel it, but I have to be strong for my son," Mary replied.

"Speaking for myself, it was saddening. I can only imagine the pain," Jess said. "What are the plans for the coming days?"

"We're planning the funeral. The police asked us to delay slightly as they did investigations. They'll give us the green light anytime now."

"Did your husband have a condition?"

"A condition? None that I knew about. If he did, he wouldn't have been able to hide it from me."

Jess wasn't totally convinced. Human beings can be cunning - even those you lived with.

"So why did they find blood pressure medication in his office?" Jess asked.

"He used to take them when he felt funny. He did it as a precaution, as the illness runs in his family," Mary explained.

Jess's eyes narrowed. "That's an odd choice. I've never heard that before."

"When he got anxious, he popped a pill. I never looked into the science but he said it was the only drug that calmed him down."

Jess made a mental note to look into the medication. "What kind of man was he?"

"Al didn't always do things like other people. That's the secret of his success. Take the motel as an example. It was a rundown place, begging for a demolition. Instead, he buys the place and transforms it into a sanctuary. He was brilliant. And then someone cuts his life short," Mary said with a tinge of disappointment.

"You believe he was murdered?"

"We curated that guest list together, to the last detail. We knew everyone. He was in great health. He never complained about feeling ill until the event. It doesn't add up that a perfectly healthy man can collapse out of the blue."

"That's why you didn't mind the police delaying the funeral," Jess said.

"Yes. I want to support them in every way possible to find my husband's killer."

"Did he have any enemies?"

"I'm not sure if these two are enemies, but they weren't on good terms with Al when he died. The first is Luan Wemba, his business partner. They fell out a few weeks ago over something and it got terrible. They were going to fight for the business. The other person is a fellow called Samkelo. I don't know his other name," Mary replied.

"Who's Samkelo?" Jess asked.

"It's a long story. But basically he's an old acquaintance of Al's who keeps popping into our lives, accusing my husband of conning him to build his business empire."

"Did it happen?"

Mary shrugged. "I hadn't met him when they did business together. But I know Al gave him some cash and he thought it was over. But he's kept coming back, keeping track of all our investments. He then makes calls or sends messages asking for his money."

"He sounds entitled.".

"And dangerous," Mary added.

"How come?" Jess asked.

"He's made death threats countless times."

"He's that committed to his madness?"

"You have no idea. I wouldn't be surprised if he was in town as we speak."

"That would be something. I can look for him," Jess blurted out, and realised her error. "I'm sorry."

"No, it's fine. I told the police about him but haven't heard from them since about it," Mary said. "It makes me uneasy."

"If he had something to do with it, he might have skipped town. Do you have a phone number or other details he used to reach you?"

Mary shook her head. "He changes numbers often. I don't think he even has a home address. People keep saying that friends offer him accommodation everywhere he goes."

Jess pursed her lips. "That's too bad. Anyway, I need to head out now. Thanks for having me."

"Thanks for the chat. It's helped ease things somewhat," Mary said.

When she got back to her car, Jess sat in the driver's seat for a few minutes, thinking about the conversation that had just taken place.

Mary was genuinely grieving over the loss, although Jess wished she'd asked her why she was the first person to find him. Had she accompanied him to the room? Had she noticed something odd in the room or about anything else around Al?

She needed to ask her these questions when they met next. But when would that be? She'd figure it out. For now, Jess knew she needed to talk to Luan and Samkelo.

Luan would be easy to track down. She assumed he worked at the company offices next to Al's office. All she had to do was get the office's physical address.

But that was just the simple part. How would she get him to talk to her? She brainstormed about this and settled on an idea: she had to fake it. During her younger years as an intern lawyer, she'd interact with council inspectors. She learned they need to regularly check on both the project site and legal documents a developer had. For this visit, she resolved to present herself as a town council inspector doing a routine visit.

She fired up the engine and drove off, buoyed by the new idea. It was something she'd never done before, but she was confident she could pull it off. One benefit of her gigantic size was that people trusted her easily. It brought a sense of authority, which she was often careful to use for good. Doing this was pushing the envelope to places she'd not been to.

But Samkelo posed a unique challenge. He was elusive and unpredictable. The fact he appeared to couch surf in friends' homes in each town he passed through meant tracking him would be difficult.

Samkelo's habit of appearing just when Al had made an enormous investment meant he was an opportunist and professional stalker. Jess again wished she'd asked Mary for some threats he had sent them.

The thought crossed her mind that it might be easier for him to find her than the reverse.

Who knows, he might even follow her home. This made her more paranoid, and suddenly every light behind her became the predatory hunter who could strike his prey at any time.

10

The next day, Jess was dressed up in the most formal dress she had, a dark brown skirt suit, a pair of stockings and black flat shoes. She had baked and packed some cookies the previous night. She'd found the address to Al's property business, AR Properties, which was in the town's small commercial business district where the main storied buildings were located. It was going to be a fifteen minute drive.

On the way there, she rehearsed talking like a town council inspector. She repeated the names of various documents: architectural plans, fire inspection certificate and various clearances and licences.

They didn't shape the Apricot Tower where the AR offices were located like an egg. But it was the only building in the town with an all glass facade despite being only three stories high. It charged the highest commercial rents, so the businesses in it were high achievers.

Jess took the lift to the third floor and walked out to the reception of AR Properties. It was an all-white reception with red highlights here and there. A large, embossed outline of the company name and logo covered the wall in front of the reception desk. A young woman in her twenties, dressed in an all blue trousers, stood up and smiled at the towering Jess.

"Welcome to AR Properties. How may I help you?" the receptionist asked.

"I'd like to see Mr. Luan," Jess said.

"Do you have an appointment?"

"No, but let him know that it's about the Dreams Motel."

"Are you a reporter or? We don't take news queries about that," the woman explained.

"No, I'm here to talk about its inspection. Just let him know that," Jess said, keeping herself professional and vague.

The receptionist hesitated, then picked up the desk phone. "Who should I say you are?"

"Just Jessica will do just fine."

The receptionist relayed the request, and there was a delay before the call ended. "He'll see you right now. Let me walk you to his office. "

Jess followed the receptionist down the hallway lined by a glass-walled office to one with the label Luan Wemba, CFO.

The receptionist held the door open. "Welcome."

Jess got in, and the door closed behind her with a distinct click sound.

The moment Jess walked into the spacious office that overlooked the town, its pricey simplicity awed her. It had light grey modular furniture that all seemed to connect into one design language. It shaped two seats like leaves, and the other like an open peapod. The table itself was a glass top shaped to mimic the map of South Africa. It made her feel out of touch with trends, these fancy designs.

Luan was standing next to the tables, smiling. He wore a pair of cotton trousers, a grey fitting sweater. He looked sharp, yet the scar on his forehead hinted at a tough upbringing.

Immediately she saw his face, Jess knew her act wouldn't work. She confirmed this when his smile faded, replaced by narrowed eyes and pursed lips.

"You said you're here about an inspection?" Luan asked. "Because I could swear on my mother's grave that I've seen you before."

He had a way with words, she could tell. He was also right, because he had seen her serving guests at the Dreams Motel launch a few days earlier. She also remembered serving him four hotdogs, which he wolfed down with gusto. Behind the sharp, lean exterior was a man who loved his food. She had to think fast.

"She said inspection? Maybe she misheard me. I didn't mean that. I said I was here to talk about the reception we had the other day."

"You mean the launch?"

"Yes, the launch. I was serving bites that day," Jess said without telling him she remembered his antics.

Luan smiled again. "Yes, you were the hotdog lady. Thank you for those. They filled me properly."

Jess smiled, more out of relief than appreciation. "You're welcome, my son. How's your day going?"

"Very good," Luan said, pointing at a leaf-shaped seat. "Please, have a seat."

Jess eyed the seat with scepticism. "Are you sure that one will manage it? I don't want to break anything here."

"They made the frame of forged steel. It's not going to break in a hundred years, I assure you. Please."

Jess sat in the seat and was amazed by how comfortable it was. "Oh my, this is lovely. Forged steel, you said? *Wena*, I want one like this."

Luan smiled as he sat in his office chair. "We imported them from outside, so it's not going to be easy to find. So, what did you want to discuss about the reception?"

"First, let me say sorry for your loss. Al Rocki was a good man."

"Yes, he was. We'll miss him, but we shall pick up the pieces and continue his good work."

He didn't sound sad to Jess, but he wasn't cold either. He knew how to hide his emotions well.

"I also wanted to give this as a thank you gift for the opportunity," Jess said as she handed him the pack of baked cookies. "I hope after this is over, we can work together again."

"Well, it's a tough week for us here, as you can understand. So we've put on hold all the events we had until we take Al to his final resting place. But things return to normal - no, nothing will be normal since Al's gone. But once we resume, we'll get in touch. Remind me of your name?"

She might've mentioned it during the launch, but Jess didn't remember.

"It's Jess. My company is Yummy Bites, down on Main Street. Those cookies will give you another idea of our variety," Jess said.

"I still daydream about those hotdogs. During these times, you hang on to those memories."

"It was so sudden. Where were you when it happened?"

"I was on the far end of the banquet room, taking a phone call. Work sometimes follows you to the social places. It's not very healthy, but it has to be done."

"You and Al started this place together?"

Luan nodded. "Yes. We've been at it for a while. We didn't start here, but a vision has brought us here."

"Who was he to you?"

Luan leaned back, eyes lifted to the ceiling. "He was a good friend. A confidant. Almost a brother. A sharp mind in the deal making rooms. I don't think I could've chosen a better business partner."

Jess found his words an interesting contrast to what Mary had told her. "Did you always get along?"

"We had our moments. Some good, some terrible. But we always fixed things."

"Did you talk much at the event? At least those memories are worth holding on to."

Luan fidgeted in his seat. "We chatted briefly. He was busy with the event. I was handling other business affairs behind the scenes."

"Did you see any sign he was ill when you talked? I found him full of energy, so I'm surprised."

"Well, I saw the same version you did. But I know he was taking some blood pressure medication, although I know he didn't really have high blood pressure. I wonder if it triggered a critical reaction."

"Oh, he took that? I'm not sure that was a good idea," Jess said as she scanned the room. She noticed one of the tall glass walls had a door. Through it she could see dumbbells, a weights rack, a Smith machine and a treadmill.

"Is that a gym?" Jess asked, pointing in that direction.

Luan followed her gaze. "Ah, yes. It can get boring working at the desk for long hours. Having my gym here helps me stay in shape."

"Wow. Does everyone have one?"

Luan chuckled. "We don't have enough room for it. Al's office is on the other side, so we share the same gym. We have another one built for the rest of the staff on the second floor."

"I'm amazed. In our days, you'd never see something like this," She scanned the room again and her eyes fell on a water bottle propped up on the table. "Is that for your water as you work or exercise?"

"Both, actually. Right now, it contains the energy drink I make at home. All organic," Luan said.

Jess remembered Detective Meyer's words about briacolite. Did he use it? "I was so impressed by the work you did at the Dreams Motel. I hope you all pull through this."

"We will. Despite all the challenges with the state of the house, the neighbours and the Baron's kids, we created something memorable that travellers can enjoy," Luan said.

Jess frowned. "Wait. You had problems with the Baron's children about the property?"

"Yes. Al found them very difficult to deal with. He never gave me the full details. Still, he sealed the deal and we own the place."

This was the first time Jess was hearing about the Baron's children. She wasn't sure it mattered. She feigned a smile. "I wish I had one of those. To keep fit. You know, in our business, it's very easy to gain weight if you keep tasting every batch of cookies you make."

"We all have to start somewhere," Luan said.

"How about we start with the recipe for that energy drink?" Jess said. "Could please write it down for me, my child?"

Luan scrambled for a pen. "Sure."

He found the pen and paper and jotted a list. He handed it to her. Jess smiled and rose to leave.

"Until next time," Jess said.

Luan reached into his card holder and handed her a business card. "Thanks for dropping by. I look forward to talking again."

As Jess left, she had a spring in her step. She was careful to say 'thank you' to the receptionist before reaching the lift.

Alone inside the lift, she unfurled the list.

2 cups water

Lemon zest
1tbsp Honey
2 bananas
½ spoon briacolite powder

She didn't read further. She carefully wrapped the piece of paper in a serviette and put it between the pages of a novel. Jess knew she had her first clue. Luan could be the prime suspect they'd been looking for all along.

11

As Jess drove, she felt a tinge of excitement. Maybe it was the adrenaline still pumping in her system after what she'd just attempted.

"Good girl for thinking fast," Jess said to herself. "That could've gone worse."

She toyed with the idea of calling Detective Meyer and tell him her suspicions. Mary said that Al and Luan were fighting for the company. But having spoken to him, it felt like the opposite was true. Luan showed no signs of a strained relationship with Al. Or was he now at ease since Al was gone? Possibly.

The gym that he shared with Al was a curious find. Jess had never imagined such a thing could be possible. She imagined the two business partners working out together, sharing stories. They would've learned each other's physical strengths and weaknesses over time. Maybe Al even confided in Luan about his high blood pressure worries. Luan seemed like the detailed type who prepared their own organic meals.

She even imagined he'd like her to make sugar free versions of her baked treats. Did Luan already know what would kill Al?

She was still unsure about these things, and maybe it would be premature to share her thoughts with Detective Meyer. He'd need more evidence than mere thoughts, right?

Maybe she should've created a distraction and then stolen the water bottle. What kind of distraction? She couldn't think of one. Maybe have him give her a tour of the mini gym? Ah yes, that could've worked. Should she turn back? No, that would raise his suspicions. But it would've been great if the police got their hands on that energy drink to test its contents.

No, stealing would be a mistake. She'd be committing a crime, especially if it turned out to be wrong. It's better if the police did it themselves, just like they did with her baked treats.

Her eyes widened in realisation. She didn't need the water bottle. She already had the ingredients in his own handwriting. That was a start, right? She'd wrapped it up to avoid messing it up with her fingerprints.

Jess slowed down and pulled over to the side of the road. She took out her mobile phone and dialled.

"Hello," Will's groggy voice said.

"Will, you're still asleep at this time?" Jess asked. It was midmorning.

"I'm awake. Just letting my body reboot."

"Reboot? Don't be lazy, son. Time is something you'll never get back. Anyway, I need your help. Instead of playing games all day, can you use your computer to do some research for me? Go on the internet and look up places that sell briacolite powder. Make a list and then let me know. Okay?" Jess said.

"Sure, Mum."

"Get on it right now. I'll be expecting it in the next hour," Jess said. "Thanks."

She hung up and got back on the road. When Jess arrived at the bakery, she caught the pleasant scent of almonds in the air.

"Please tell me you're making an almond croissant," Jess said. The doorbell jingled as it closed behind her.

Lerato grinned. "I am making croissants, but they're not for you."

"You know our unwritten rule: when making those, always add three extra for me," Jess said. She considered almond croissants, with their soft insides coated in honey, as the best snack in the world.

"There's a reason it's unwritten. It's not meant to be remembered."

"Is that so?" Jess said as she walked up to where Lerato had laid out half a dozen. Their freshness was too much to resist, and she grabbed one and bit into it.

"*Anti*! I told you to keep off!" Lerato lamented. "That's a client's order. "

"I'll help you make another," Jess said, her voice muffled as she chewed. She closed her eyes, savouring the taste. "Mmh, mm, mm!"

Lerato shook her head. "Are you from the courtroom looking like that? Didn't you have breakfast today?"

"No, I'm from a meeting. And I actually never had breakfast at home."

"The saying goes 'don't eat your own stock - unless you want to close shop.'"

"I'll heed your advice after one more," Jess said, reaching for another. She got to it before Lerato could slap her hand away. "Where's Penny?"

"She's gone to the wholesalers to buy supplies," Lerato said. "Now get away from my work space before we fight."

Jess chuckled and moved to the cash counter. She sat on the high stool, watching Lerato work.

"I was thinking about the Baron family," Jess began. "I have to agree with you. I find them odd."

Lerato beamed. "I told you that you'd come round."

"Don't get your hopes up. I'm still unconvinced about the curse stuff. But Henry Baron, the man who built that house, was quite wealthy when he died. He owned some of the largest vineyards in the country, and Baron Wines was employing lots of people in the town. What happened?"

"The kids happened," Lerato replied. "They killed off that empire brick by brick until it was on its knees."

"I've seen the factory outside town that was shut down years ago. It was a pretty huge operation in its day."

"Like you said, you couldn't find a family that hadn't worked directly or indirectly for Baron Wines. He used to pay people well, too."

"So why is it that people talk more about the curse of the house instead of the good things his business brought?"

"He was an odd man. He was very generous and working for him felt like the best thing in the world. Very sharp, he had an uncanny eye for detail. Although he was generous, he could hardly sustain a conversation. He'd listen to you and help you. That was it. So, at the end of the day, no one really knew him," Lerato said.

"That sounds like any ordinary introvert with a good heart."

"There's more. People knew his kids, oddly named Prince and Precious, but no one had ever seen their mother. They kept to themselves much more than he did. Then people started noticing strange people in long cloaks coming to his house every Saturday evening. This wasn't your regular priest. They'd spend the night there and leave on Sunday morning. People who passed there at night would hear chanting. But no one knew what it was all about," Lerato said.

"I have a feeling that's when the curse rumours started," Jess said.

"Partially. His death really triggered them. It was a Friday, and he'd actually done a staff lunch where he gave cash gifts and promotions. Everyone was glad. Then when he went home, he apparently fell down the stairs and broke his neck during the night. He died. People believed it at first. But when the kids refused to conduct a postmortem, and then moved out of the house after he was cremated, everyone got suspicious," Lerato said.

"Why didn't they want a postmortem done?"

"He apparently had a history of sleepwalking, and people had previously met him walking down the country road at night. So maybe it was going to happen eventually," Lerato said. "Then strange things started happening at the house."

"Strange things like what?"

"They'd hear the wails of a man. The others say they'd see a man peeking through one window as if asking for help. It was strange. That's when people started saying his spirit was restless, haunting the house."

"And that the spirit will do anything to get people's attention."

"Yes. Perhaps his ghost wants justice for his death."

Jess sighed, rubbing the side of her temple. "It all sounds a bit much, don't you think?"

Lerato shrugged. "I'm just telling you what's happened. Even homeless people who spent the night there said they felt a strange energy in the palace. Maybe the same energy I felt when Al died."

"I think the one thing that everyone is curious about is his lifestyle, and that everyone wonders if he truly died from a fall. The kids not doing a postmortem didn't help."

"Now look, they've ruined everything he built. The name Baron isn't what it used to be."

"Where do they live?" Jess asked.

"I've been told their father bought a hill outside town. There's a vast ranch there. They keep to themselves, but sometimes you see them in town."

"It almost sounds like they never wanted to be a part of this community," Jess said. "Have you seen the kids? What are they like?"

"I've only seen them once, two years ago. They were walking in town with two of their friends, all looking posh. I think they're both nearing their thirties. Prince is the firstborn, Precious the second. Prince looks talkative, while his sister is like her father, observing everything while hardly talking."

"What do you think caused them to want to stay away, other than the rumours?"

"They wanted to milk the business without people questioning them. People would lose their jobs but would find it hard to talk to them. While their father would walk the streets, greet people and listen to them without talking much, these two wanted nothing to do with anyone. In less than a decade, it reduced the biggest name in town to a byword," Lerato replied.

After that brief description, the Baron siblings weren't people Jess wanted to meet. But she was now curious about them. She had to get to them.

12

Jess was at the bakery, finishing up on a batch of strawberry cupcakes, when a nervous Tau called.

"Can you talk for a minute?" Tau asked.

"Sure. Are you okay?" Jess asked.

"I could be better. I got a call from Samkelo. He threatened me."

"He what?"

"He threatened me. He wants the money Dad owed him - five million rand. I don't have five million rand."

Jess whistled. "That's a lot of money. What did he threaten to do?"

"He didn't give specifics. He just said that now that my father is out of the way, it should be easier. If I don't listen then, he said 'karma will find justice.' I have no idea what that means, but I know he plans to harm me," Tau said.

"Where are you now?"

"I was about to head home from Dad's office," Tau said.

"Meet me at the same place as last time. Let's talk some more. Watch your back in case someone's following you," Jess said.

She hung up and took off her apron. She turned to Penny, who was helping her.

"Hey, I've got to head out and meet someone. You can make sure the last batch comes out, okay? No fires."

"My phone is no longer on me when we're baking, so they'll be fine," Penny said.

Jess smiled. "Great. I'll be back soon."

She drove to the Chess Restaurant and was there in less than twenty minutes. She arrived before him and was glad that it wasn't as full as last time. So she chose a cubicle on the ground floor section, which offered more privacy and had better ventilation.

As she waited, she ordered Rooibos tea. By the time the reddish beverage arrived five minutes later, Tau hadn't arrived yet. She thought of calling him, since his office wasn't too far from the restaurant. What was keeping him? She opted to wait ten more minutes.

She sipped the tea, her taste buds relishing the woody flavour it had.

She saw Tau's form walk through the main door and approach her. As he searched for her, she waved at him. He scuttled to her cubicle and sat down across from her.

"Thanks for coming," Tau said.

"No, thank you for calling me. How was the drive?" Jess asked.

"Stressful. I thought someone was following me so I took a detour and got into some traffic. It was a false alarm."

"I was wondering why you were taking so long. But glad you're here. What will you have?" Jess asked.

"Just a lemonade," Tau said. Jess signalled the waiter who took his order.

"So, have you told the police about this?"

Tau shook his head. "He told me not to. He called it the out of court settlement he never got."

"Be honest with me: do you think your father did anything wrong for this guy to follow him all this time?"

"I've had the same question each time he resurfaces. I've done my research behind my father's back. Dad already settled with him. The problem is Samkelo says he was short changed since we used our valuer to assess the land. He got another valuer who quoted a higher valuation for the property, and now wants more money. My dad said no, and it's been a back and forth ever since," Tau said.

Jess wanted to believe him, but it seemed like Samkelo had a justified reason to claim more cash. But perhaps his means of recovering the money was the problem. "Has he ever hurt either of you before?"

"Physically? No. Mentally? Yeah. Reputation-wise? Initially. People now consider him a rabble-rouser," Tau said. "But I can't shake off the fact that his voice was a bit more sinister this time."

Jess raised a brow. "What made it more sinister?"

"His tone. His slow drawl as he spoke. He's usually loud and rambling. But this time his speech was more controlled, like he knows a lot more than I do. It was unnerving."

"I know what you mean. I'm curious to hear it for myself," Jess said.

"He always calls with a different number and deactivates it afterwards. He calls you, not the other way round."

"Unpredictable," Jess said and leaned forward. "But I want to assure you that nothing will happen to you."

Tau just sighed, as if he found it difficult to receive the comforting words.

"Tell me about Baron's kids. You met them when your father was buying the House of Baron, right? How old are they?"

Tau nodded. "Yeah, I met them. They looked like they were in their late twenties so they should now turn thirty or there-abouts. They were opposites of each other. Prince is the first-born. A big talker. He had many ideas about what we should do with the place, but many were impractical. He was just selling the place to get the best value for money. His sister Precious is soft-spoken. Between them, I'd say she's the brains. She's quiet most of the time before surprising you with a deep insight. But they were both very keen about the House of Baron getting a new lease of life. Precious had more questions and didn't offer any ideas about what to do with the place. She seemed sceptical about my Dad."

"Was the sale smooth sailing?" Jess asked.

"It was done within a month of the offer, but there were lots of emails and calls exchanged. We almost gave up on the deal but Prince pushed it through," Tau said. "He really wanted it done and dusted."

"I was trying to see if they had any conflicts with your father about the sale. So they didn't have a bone to pick with your father?"

Tau shook his head. "No. I mainly dealt with Prince, and he was eager to sell. Precious had tons of questions but didn't oppose things in a way to suggest she wasn't happy. I guess people want to be assured their sentimental property will be in safe hands."

"And have they come back to see the property? You could've invited them to the launch."

"That was purely transactional. We owed them nothing after we bought the place. We changed it in a way they hadn't managed to, so Dad didn't find it necessary."

"Your father was a warm man, but he didn't play around with business."

"No, and he taught us to think on our feet and think five steps ahead."

"I know it can't be easy at this time," she said.

"It's not. But I'm not going to let what he built wither away."

Jess admired his conviction. He'd probably seen what the Baron siblings had done with their father's inheritance, and was learning from their oversights.

They kept chatting about other things as Tau shared more about his father. Jess learned he was a football fan who supported Orlando Pirates at home and Manchester United in England. As a club member, he was due to receive fresh jerseys from both teams next week but that wasn't to be.

Jess gave Tau the best advice she could about handling Samkelo, including when to ask for help from the police.

When they parted ways, he was in higher spirits than when he arrived.

She made sure he had driven off, and no one was following before she got into her car.

She had one phone call to make before she headed back to the bakery.

"Hello, Will? How's your day going?" Jess asked.

"It's great," Will replied in his now customary slow drawl.

"I forgot to call you earlier about the research. How far have you gone?"

Will released an agonised groan. "Oh, man."

Jess' eyes narrowed. "What's wrong?"

"Er… Well, it kind of slipped my mind. But I'll get to it right after this call."

Jess felt a hot flush on her cheeks. She clenched the steering wheel. "What on earth have you been doing? You've had lots of time to finish it."

"I got distracted."

"Distracted by what, Will? Are you working from home?"

"Well, I've done a few chores…"

"That's not work. Are you working from home for your mind to be that distracted? Or is it the video game again?" Jess prodded.

"Calm down, Mum. I'll get to it right after this."

"You better. And you know what? I think you should get yourself a proper job. You clearly need some routine in your life. Or maybe you could live with one of your sisters for a few months?"

"You don't have to be that drastic."

"But I do. If you can't help me around, then I think you might benefit with a change of pace," Jess said. "You remember at what age your sisters moved out?"

Will hesitated. "I don't remember."

"Faith was 28 and Lesedi was 27. And when they graduated they spent their days poring through the classified sections looking for jobs and volunteer positions. I'm pretty sure you're not doing that, right?"

"I've been working on that too Mum. Okay, I'm sorry I forgot about this. Give me time to make it up to you. Please," Will said.

"You have an hour."

"I'm on it," Will said and hung up.

Jess shook her head. She felt disrespected and wasn't going to let it go. If she was too lenient, he'd be emboldened to keep lazing around, and she'd have to pick up the slack after him. Besides, she'd made too many sacrifices since their father left. She wasn't going to let any of them fail. All of them had to make it in life. If a scolding would help achieve that, then so be it.

She lowered the window and took a few deep breaths until she calmed down. She switched on the car, ready to drive when her phone rang again. It was Penny.

"Jess, I need your help," Penny said.

"What's going on?"

"It's my husband. I can't take it anymore, so I'm doing the meeting tomorrow," Penny said.

"The meeting?"

"Yes, the one I told you to help me with. Please, if I don't do this tomorrow it will be over for this marriage. Please, come and help me," Penny pleaded.

Jess knew it was a bad idea for her to go. It might trigger terrible memories. But she couldn't say no, either.

"Sure. You know I can't let you down," Jess said, half believing her own words.

13

Jess drove back to the bakery and found Penny had finished packing the cupcakes. They talked about the next day's mediation event, and Jess felt even more out of place. She'd been single for so long that talking about marriage problems wasn't part of her reality. She'd take comfort in the fact that Lerato was tagging along.

When she got home later that night, she checked on Will, and he managed to sweet talk his way into a time-extension for the research.

The next morning, he gave her a list of four pharmacies that were within Fort Bay. They were all small pharmacies that she'd not used before. Two were in the same part of the town while the other two were in separate locations.

"I was wondering why you'd want to learn about the chemical. Do you want to start working out?" Will asked.

"Maybe I want to start an energy drink line," Jess said with a wink.

"I don't believe you."

"Would you sell it if I made it?"

"I'm no salesman, Mum."

"You might want to be one, seeing as you've not bagged a job yet."

Will shook his head and walked away. Jess was amused. She was getting results. That's when she got an idea about Samkelo. She reached for her phone and called Tau, asking him to meet her at the bakery.

He arrived at mid-morning and Jess took him for a walk.

"I think it's important that I meet Samkelo. He might know something about the case," Jess said.

"How do you plan to do that?" Tau asked.

Jess remained silent, looking at him. Tau read her mind and shook his head.

"No, I'm not going to do that," Tau said.

"All you have to do is tell him you'd want to meet him face to face first," she said.

"Doing that means we'll have to go with cash. That won't happen."

"But you can raise the money, right?"

Tau sighed and shook his head. "My father wouldn't want that. I can't do it. Besides, meeting him is a gamble we can't take. He's unpredictable."

"Listen. I know it's risky, but we can make him think that we have the money. If he tries something funny, we can make him think he's surrounded. We can use those bluffs as our leverage," Jess said.

"How do you know how he'll react to it?"

"I don't. But I can ask a detective what to do."

"He doesn't want the police involved."

"I'll ask him as if it's all in my imagination," Jess suggested.

Tau sighed. "I'll have to think about it."

"Fair enough. Give it some thought and then we can see what to do. The sooner the better," Jess said.

After that, Tau left.

Later that day, Jess and Lerato arrived in Midville, a middle class neighbourhood in the west side of the town. The homes were all in bungalow style with individual compounds, tall gates and high fences. A few cars were parked outside Penny's gate, signalling there were other guests inside.

"This thing is usually for the relatives and neighbours, right?" Jess asked Lerato after they found a parking spot.

"*Eish*, but we're like sisters to her, or what are you trying to say?" Lerato asked.

"True. I'm just trying to make sure our presence won't raise the tension."

"Why would it? You're just nervous. Relax, I'm here and will show you the ropes," Lerato said with a sly grin.

Jess sighed and got out of the car. They walked to the tall dark green gate and went in through the small door for walk-in visitors. They found themselves in a large front lawn. On it were fourteen chairs: twelve arranged in a semi-circle manner and the two remaining ones were at the top of the semicircle. All the seats were empty.

"*Yhoo*, this is serious," Lerato said.

They spotted Penny walking towards them. She wore a colourful dress with Zulu patterns on the fabric. She gave a tired smile as she came to them.

"Glad to see you guys," Penny said. "Come and sit here."

She led them to the left side of the semi-circle. Penny sat on the last two seats on that row.

"Are we the only people here?" Jess asked.

"There are other guests inside. I'm only waiting for a few more before we begin," Penny said.

"So how's it going to go?" Lerato asked.

"Families of both sides will be here. My husband and I. Then we're going to be mediated by an elder. He'll listen to both sides and then give us a solution that works for both of us," Penny said.

"So we just hang in here and offer you moral support," Lerato said.

"If something about work comes up, then you'll speak up for me."

"Oh, we'll do that. Don't worry about that," Lerato said, "Right, Jess?"

Jess smiled. "Oh yes, we're with you all the way,"

"Thanks. That means a lot to me," Penny said.

Minutes later, three other guests arrived from Penny's family and the rest came out of the main house.

Penny's guests sat on the left while her husband Lawrence's guests were on the right. The elder, a grey-haired man with a multicolour scarf around his neck and an ornately carved walking stick, took charge of the proceedings.

"My name is Elder Sizwe. We're here at the invitation of our children Lawrence and Penny. They have matters which we would like to help them overcome," the elder said, his eyes roving left and right. "We're not here to spread gossip or malicious lies. What we say here is entrusted to us and whatever peace will come from it will be our blessing. Ubuntu is here with us. I am because we are. So let us begin."

As culturally important as this was, Jess couldn't help wondering why Penny didn't do marriage counselling. This felt like a kangaroo court.

However, she knew her thoughts didn't come because she hated the idea. She was impatient. She had a case to attend to, and she was itching to figure out how to outsmart Samkelo and possibly coax him into meeting and talking with her.

Lawrence stated his testimony. He spoke about how he spent more time at home after losing his job. Although he had enough savings, he felt Penny was treating him with disdain.

"She doesn't help me with the chores like she used to. She even struggles to hug me as she leaves for work in the morning. A man needs his woman to show some affection," Lawrence said.

"Is this true, Penny?" Elder Sizwe asked.

"I have late nights and early mornings a lot of times these days. So maybe we don't have the affection we used to have, but it's not because I don't respect him," Penny replied. "I'm just wondering why he drinks so much. Each day I come home he's smelling of alcohol. It gets hard to hug someone if that's the smell I deal with."

There were murmurs amongst the group.

"Let's maintain silence, please," Elder Sizwe said authoritatively. "Lawrence, what is this with the drink?"

"I have stopped. It was happening at first. But even she can tell you I have reduced. Right?" Lawrence said.

"He reduced after I asked him about the woman," Penny said.

"What woman is this?" Elder Sizwe asked.

"There is no woman," Lawrence countered. "She's saying this because she was making me special cookies the other day and took them to another man!"

Penny stood up. "They got burnt in the oven. Even the fire department came to the bakery."

"I didn't see it in the news," Lawrence replied.

Lerato shot up. "She's telling the truth. We work with her. Don't we, Jess?"

Lerato pulled Jess up by the arm. Of course, Jess being much larger wasn't going to come up with a mere tug. But it compelled her to stand by her friends. Jess had no choice but to join in.

"Yes, we do," Jess said. "She's telling the truth."

Lawrence shot up too. "Elder, why has she brought imposters to our meeting?"

Lerato didn't hold back. "Who are you calling an imposter?"

Then a shouting match where many voices joined in ensued. Jess shook her head in disbelief.

14

Jess tried to have Lerato sit back down, but Lerato wasn't having it. "This man can't disrespect us like that."

"We don't have to make it worse than it already is," Jess said amid the cacophony of voices.

"Don't be soft," Lerato said.

But Jess wasn't being soft. She meant every word. Watching the confusion reign, she decided to use her other weapon: her voice.

"Can we all calm down? You, calm down," Jess bellowed, turning to one side. She turned to another. "Calm down!"

Her voice and her towering frame made people stop talking while others lowered their tones. In seconds, the noise died down.

"I think it will be wise if we all take a quick break and then we'll return here after ten minutes. Let's be careful with our words when we return," Elder Sizwe said. He rose and retreated to the house, followed by some relatives. Penny came to Jess and Lerato, and they walked out to Jess's car.

"You see what I mean?" Penny spoke as a tear rolled down her cheek. "This is over for us."

It tempted Jess to encourage her, but she felt it would sound hollow.

Lerato shook her head. "No, it's not. You're both fighting the symptoms instead of the cause."

"What do you mean?" Penny asked.

"I was once in a similar situation with my husband. We'd argue over tiny things. We'd never spend a waking moment without questioning each other. But the problem wasn't the minor faults we noticed about each other. It was the fact we didn't spend enough time with each other. Also, I had just started the bakery with Jess and we'd do 12-hour shifts. This wasn't great for the marriage," Lerato said.

"So you're saying our problem is time together?" Penny asked.

Jess was listening, but had also just received a text. Tau had just spoken to Samkelo and had set up a meeting for later that afternoon. Her heart raced with excitement.

"Your husband lost his job and is now home most of the time. He's not used to that, but money is also not a problem at the moment. However, you're also not used to that. Have you ever sat down and talked to each other about the situation? Like in depth?" Lerato asked.

Penny shook her head. "No, I haven't. I didn't even know he had savings."

"You see? He isn't worried about it, but you are. And there's tension between the two of you for different reasons. You need to have that talk."

Penny nodded. "Okay, I see what you mean."

As they spoke, Jess' mind was elsewhere. She was worried about meeting Samkelo later.

"You'll be fine, Penny. Guys, excuse me for a second. I need to make a phone call," Jess said.

She walked away from the two and called Detective Meyer. "Hello Detective, how's your day going?"

"I'm well. How may I help you?" Detective Meyer replied.

"I had a hypothetical question: if someone was going to meet someone who's blackmailing them, do you think they should go with someone else or not?"

"Is this from a novel?"

"Something like that."

"Well, it's best if they don't meet them. Don't negotiate with anyone blackmailing you," Meyer said.

"What if you have to?"

"These things are best handled by the professionals. Don't go alone. Don't try to be a hero," Meyer replied. "Is this hypothetical?"

"Yes, it is. Thanks for the insight."

"Okay. If it isn't hypothetical, don't do or say anything crazy," the detective warned.

"I hear you, but there's nothing to worry about," Jess insisted.

She hung up and walked back to Penny and Lerato. They were ready to go back in. They returned, and the mediation continued for another hour. By the time it was over, it was agreed that the couple would talk about the change in their circumstances. But they were going to stay together and create time for each other.

Jess and Lerato left a relieved Penny as they headed to the bakery. Jess felt a buzz inside.

Later that afternoon, Jess drove with Tau towards the address he'd been given. It wasn't a long drive to the taxi rank, which was lined with various minivans waiting for passengers to take home during rush hour.

They drove past the rank and went behind it, where several warehouses were. Most were abandoned. They looked for warehouse 12, which was at the end of the line. Jess turned the car and parked it such that it faced the exit road.

"Let me see if he's here," Tau said.

"You're not going out there alone," Jess said, opening the driver's door. "There's no money to keep safe."

Tau didn't complain. They split up, with Tau checking the side door and Jess walking around the warehouse.

She noted the iron sheet walls were thick but rusted. She saw empty pallets thrown against the walls, looking weathered out by the elements. A broken down forklift was also parked near the perimeter wall.

"There's no one here," Tau said behind her.

"Seems like he's running late. Or watching us from somewhere."

"Watching us?" Tau asked, looking up towards the roofs.

"Don't mind me. I've watched one too many TV shows," Jess replied.

Then they heard a motorcycle engine in the distance. The sound got louder until they saw it bearing down on them.

"Walk to the car," Jess said as she nudged Tau forward. They were next to the car doors when the lone rider stopped some metres away from them. He wore a black and white helmet, a dark leather jacket, and pants. He turned to them and stared, not taking off his helmet. Jess got nervous.

"Is that you?" Tau asked.

"Where's the money?" the rider asked in a muffled voice.

"I need to confirm that it's you first."

The rider said nothing and for a moment Jess feared he'd draw a gun and shoot them. She remembered the Detective's words: don't do anything crazy.

After a tense yet brief wait, the rider got off his bike and took off the helmet. It was a bearded man with short hair and chapped lips. He stared at Tau.

"Happy now?" Samkelo asked.

"Is that him?" Jess asked.

Tau nodded. "Yeah, it's him."

"Where's my money?" Samkelo asked, walking towards Tau. He had a way of speaking that made his mouth snarl and his eyes glaze.

Tau opened the car door just in case he needed to jump in. Jess was wary that even if they got in, Samkelo could use the helmet to break in the windows and get to them. She also still wasn't sure if he didn't have a firearm. They'd have to talk him down.

"You're late," Jess said.

Samkelo turned to her. "Who are you, Mama?"

"Tau's sidekick."

"You should stay out of this. I have respect for you."

"We kept the money elsewhere," Jess said.

Samkelo glared at her. "You what? We agreed you'd have it here."

"Yes, but it's a lot of money. We can't carry all of it in this neighbourhood."

"Where is it? Let's go or I'll have to do something you don't like."

"I'd like you to tell me a few things first. Where were you when the Dreams Motel launch was happening?"

"I was riding my bike on the highways."

"Were you riding with anyone?"

"I ride alone. Why do you want to know?" Samkelo asked.

"I just thought you'd attend it, since you knew Tau's father," Jess said.

"They didn't invite me. Now let's stop the stories and give me the money."

"It was impossible to get the money from Al. But now that he's out of the way, to use your own words, you want Tau to pay up, right?"

Samkelo chuckled. It was an odd, humourless laugh. "I know what game you're trying to play. You'll have to find someone who saw me in this town. No one did, because I wasn't here. Now, give me my money!"

Samkelo closed in on Tau, who jumped into the car and shut the door. Samkelo reached for the handle, but Tau had already locked it.

"Don't touch my car, otherwise the police who are watching you right now will ruin your day," Jess said.

Samkelo snarled. "I told you not to call the police."

"You thought we'd come here alone? So now you have a choice. Either you hang around and they arrest you, or you leave peacefully and maybe you'll get your money another day," Jess said.

Samkelo licked his lips, and started retreating towards his motorcycle, his eyes still trained on Jess.

"I'll be watching you," Samkelo said. He then put on his helmet, sat on his bike, and rode away.

Jess got into the car and exhaled. "He's intense."

"That he is," Tau said.

"Let's get out of here," Jess said as she switched on the car. As she drove off, she believed Samkelo knew something about Al's death. He didn't have to be here physically if he had someone on the inside to do the job for him. An assassin.

15

Jess drove around town for half an hour, making sure there wasn't a rider in a dark outfit following them. She then dropped Tau at his home before she called it a day herself.

When Jess got home, the sky was a beautiful orange as the sun headed toward the horizon. It felt calming, and she was smiling as she turned into her parking. But she stopped when she saw a battered old mini-van parked in her spot. The parking space can only accommodate one car at a time, so she had to back up and parallel park on the street.

She got into her house, ready to grill her son.

"Will?" Jess called.

"Yeah?" Will calmly replied. He was seated at the computer desk, working on the computer.

"Why is there a wreck of a car parked in my spot?"

"Oh, sorry. I didn't think you'd be back this early. Let me move it," Will said, rising to his feet. He picked a pair of keys off the table and walked to the door.

"Not so fast. Whose car is that?"

"It's mine."

"That car is yours?"

"Yes," Will said, smiling. "My first car."

Jess's eyes narrowed. "With what money?"

"Don't worry about that," Will said as he walked past her.

"How did it get here yet you don't have a driving license?"

Will hesitated. "A friend drove me here."

She didn't believe him. "You can't keep it if you don't tell me how you got it."

"I've been saving."

"What do you plan to do with it?"

"You'll see when it's ready," Will said with a wink. He then stepped out. Jess heard the car roar to life, with a louder engine than she'd heard in a long time. The van backed out of her spot.

Moments later, Will returned.

"Give me your keys. I'll park yours," he offered.

Too tired to argue, Jess obliged. For the rest of that evening, she tried to learn more about the van, but Will kept his cards close to his chest.

The next day, Jess found the address to the Baron Ranch by simply asking around. Lerato gave her a few hints, but the local grocer, who occasionally gets some vegetables from their farm, gave her the exact location. It was a forty-minute drive on the A52 highway, with rolling countryside, hills, vineyards, and a few motels rolling by.

When she was younger, Jess loved taking long drives out of town just to marvel at the beauty. Occasionally, she would take the children on those trips as family holidays and they would camp by a river or stay at one of the many hotels in the area. She didn't want them to miss out on some life experiences, even though she was raising them alone.

This was a tourist hotspot because it resembles the Garden of Eden. Perhaps that's why the Baron siblings had moved out of the town. The peace of the countryside may have helped in their healing. She looked forward to hearing from them if they let her in.

"They don't just let you in, especially if they weren't expecting you," the grocer said.

"Can you call them for me?" Jess asked. "It's really important."

After much cajoling, the grocer called them and they agreed to meet her. To return the favour, Jess bought twice the number of strawberries she usually bought from him.

As he'd told her, she came across a small hill after the Little Forest, a small clump of jacaranda trees next to the highway. They bloomed to reveal their magnificent purple flowers every April and fall, and it was always enchanting driving by them. She turned onto a gravel road and drove to a wooden gate. A uniformed guard emerged from a gatehouse, opened the gate and approached her car. He swung a club to his side.

"Can I help you?" he asked in a gruff voice.

"I'm here to see Prince and Precious," Jess said.

He gave her the once over and searched her car, from the front to the boot. It was a sign that they were expecting her. He then waved her on. She drove for a kilometre into the estate before coming across a large black gate. This one opened automatically, and she drove into the compound of a mansion. It had well landscaped bushes around it. A gardener was watering a flower bed as she parked next to two black SUVs.

When she got out, she saw that though the house was large and awe-inspiring; it needed a fresh coat of paint.

She walked to the main door. As she neared it, it opened and a young man in a white shirt and well-pressed pants came out. He smiled at her. He had an afro hairstyle, which she figured by its length and fullness, he'd kept going for at least five years.

"You're Jess?" Prince asked eloquently.

"Yes," Jess said, looking down at him. As was often the case, she was taller than the people she met, and Prince wasn't an exception. This intimidated some people, but Prince seemed amazed.

"Prince is my name, but I think you already know that. You've got to be the tallest person I've met in a few months," Prince said.

"I'll take that as a compliment," Jess said.

"You should. It rarely comes from my lips. So when it does, you run with it."

Jess caught the swagger he had. He was no pushover. She also expected him to ask her inside, but he made no attempt to do so. So they stood outside the front door, talking.

"So what brings you out here?" Prince asked.

"I enjoy taking long drives," Jess said. "I often wondered what was behind that gate. Thank you for agreeing to see me."

"The grocer is a good friend of ours in town. One of the few who can understand our needs and what we're about."

"What are you about?"

Prince chuckled. "We're about immortality. We're here to create a slice of heaven never seen before. Some people down there, in that town, don't understand that and aren't ready for it."

Jess tried not to frown. "Not ready for what?"

"For the change we're going to bring. That town will change soon."

"Are you moving back into town?"

Prince ran two fingers over his mouth as if zipping them shut. "I'll say nothing about it. I'll have to see if you're ready for it or not. Only the chosen ones need to know."

Jess found the conversation odd. So when Precious, dressed in a floral sundress and sandals, emerged, Jess was relieved.

Prince turned to his sister. "Pree, this is Jessica. She came to see what we're all about. Should we call her a local tourist?"

Precious, who was of similar height to Prince, studied Jess in silence for a few seconds.

"Hello," she said. "I'm Precious. Welcome."

"Thank you," Jess said.

Precious didn't ask her inside, either. These were two peas in a pod. "I hope my brother told you we don't do farm tours these days."

"Well, I wish I could check out the place. But I'm truly here to talk about the House of Baron."

Precious raised a brow. "Why is that important to you?"

"Well, I used to be a lawyer. As I was looking into the records, I wondered if the property transfer caused you any problems."

"No, it was smooth as melted butter," Prince said.

Jess kept her gaze on Precious.

"It worked out in the end," Precious said. "Do you have any other thing you want to talk about?"

"No, that was the main thing I had in mind," Jess said.

"We already sold it. You should talk to the new owners," Precious said.

"They can't tell me about the curse of the house."

"There's no curse," Prince said.

"Well, there have been strange things happening in the past," Jess added.

"I think you might want to leave now," Prince said, his face darkening.

"No, I think she should stay," Precious said.

"Pree, we said we'd not talk about this again."

"The past doesn't hold power over us anymore, Prince," Precious said. "It's time we showed her what's in the closet."

As ominous as that sounded, Jess wanted to see it.

16

"Skeletons?" Jess asked, tilting her head to the side.

Precious smiled. "It's a figure of speech. Come with me."

"Pree…," Prince began.

Precious cut him off. "I've got it covered, Prince."

Jess followed her as she was led through the front door.

Inside the house, the high ceiling, the all-wood finish, and the blend of modern touches with rustic elements took Jess in. The house had a smart security system and LED lighting was installed in the spaces she saw. In the living room, all the furniture was a modern styling of polished leather seats, and a high-end 72-inch television hung on the longest wall. The wood finish, the exposed trusses on the ceiling, and the red brick fireplace gave the room its old-school feel. The other thing that caught Jess' attention was the large shelf that went five shelves high, fully stacked with books of all kinds.

"Please, have a seat," Precious said as she sat on the arm of the leather couch.

Jess eased into a single seater whose leather surface felt plush and firm at the same time. Prince went and stood next to the fireplace.

Precious smiled. "You asked about the curse of the House of Baron. As Prince said, there's no such thing. At least not one that affects the locals. But if you're referring to something that has affected us as a family, then there's some truth in it."

Jess frowned. "What do you mean?"

"Our father was an odd man. I'm sure you're already aware of that. He was kind and generous, smart and innovative, but also was aloof to most people. Even we, as his kids, didn't really understand him. But he loved us, no doubt about it. And he took his time to teach us how to run a business and how to manage various properties."

Jess wasn't too sure the management lessons had been effective, judging by how the two siblings had run down their father's businesses.

Precious continued. "He sheltered us a lot from things. Looking back, I wish he hadn't protected us from the world. We would've managed his loss better. We would've kept some of his investments going. But we didn't have the full picture most of the time. When he died, we lost our anchor, and it took us a long time to recover. As we found our feet, his businesses fell apart. Then people started the rumours. It all became too much for us."

"Is that why you moved out here?" Jess asked.

Precious nodded. "We needed the space to find our footing again. It came at a price. We scaled down his investments. I now realise it wasn't the smartest thing to do."

Prince chimed in. "It was the best thing to do at the time."

"No, it wasn't," Precious retorted.

"Yes, it was! We didn't have the experience of running all those businesses."

"We could've kept some of them. Maybe we wouldn't be struggling with overheads right now."

"Sometimes it's better to count your losses and move on."

"Our inheritance isn't a loss. I hope you one day get round to understanding that," Precious said.

Prince raised his hands in mock surrender. "I don't need to. We're doing just fine right now."

Precious sighed and turned back to Jess. "We clearly see things differently, but we're taking a day at a time. It will all work out in the end."

"How did your father die, if you don't mind me asking?" Jess asked.

"He was born with a heart defect from childhood. We knew about this and did our best to look after him. It started getting worse as he got older, but we thought we still had a few years with him to put things in order. We were wrong. The day he died was the worst day of my life. I couldn't sleep for weeks after that. Each time I'd walk through the house, I'd think of him. Come to think of it, it was one of the main reasons we moved here. It was too painful to live in that house," Precious said.

Jess nodded. She could understand that sometimes even the things your loved one treasured become sources of pain after their loss. "So there was no problem you encountered while selling the house? Did anyone else want to buy it?"

"We got hundreds of other offers for the place. But we turned down all of them," Precious said.

Prince interjected. "But at some point, the right offer comes along and you can't pass it up."

"What made Al's offer the right one?" Jess asked.

"There's never a right one," Precious replied.

"It was better than all the rest. The man had a plan for renovating it and the best part was the fact he wouldn't tear it down," Prince said.

Precious shook her head in silence.

"Did you both agree on the sale?" Jess prodded.

"Yes," Prince said. Precious shrugged and nodded in resignation.

"Great. Thanks for the responses. That's all I had for today," Jess said as she rose, seeing no need for further interrogation. She fully understood why they moved out of the town, and their great appetite for privacy. People recover from pain in different ways, and this was working for them.

"What did your questions have to do with the law and permits again?" Precious asked.

"Sometimes understanding the context of a sale is much more than words on a paper. That's what I wanted to get the full idea of," Jess explained. "It's a new role and they have asked me to look into sales that happened in the last eighteen months."

Precious frowned. "I still don't get it, but okay?"

The two siblings escorted Jess to her car.

"Call me directly the next time you want to talk," Precious said, handing over a business card, which Jess didn't expect.

"I sure will."

As Jess drove out, she felt vindicated. The myths were unfounded, and had only hurt the grieving family further. Human beings often create their own hoaxes to make sense of things.

When she got to the bakery, she found a crestfallen Penny alone, kneading some dough. She did it with less vigour than usual, and Jess knew something was up.

"What's wrong, Penny?"

"He moved out of the house," Penny replied.

"He what?" Jess asked, although she'd heard her clearly.

"He moved out. He said it would be a good idea to have some space for a few days."

"And you agreed to this?"

Penny shrugged. "What more could I do?"

"Maybe he was testing to see if you really wanted to stay together."

"That doesn't work with me. Besides, maybe I wanted a break too. I just didn't know how to say it."

Jess crossed her arms. "If you really wanted a break, then why are you sulking right now?"

Penny paused, and that's when Jess saw she was about to break down. She moved her from the working area and they leaned on the front counter.

"I'm just scared. I've never done this before and I hate the uncertainty," Penny said.

"I hear you. I don't know how to give advice on how to stay together. But I have experience in how breakups start. When my ex-husband left me, it started with something similar. A break for a few days. The days we spent together became fewer than the days we spent away from each other. We drifted apart. Then one day he left town, and I never heard from him again."

"I don't want that," Penny said.

"Then don't make the same mistake. I didn't fight for our marriage. I thought it was too far gone. But yours isn't. I think you and Lawrence still love each other. If you want it to work, fight for it."

"So I should find him?"

"Yeah, talk to him. Of course, you can wait two more days. It will help both of you assess the situation. But don't let it go for more than that. Get back together and fight for your love."

"You're sounding romantic," Penny said with a smile.

Jess grinned. "Maybe I've always been one. I just haven't found my luck."

"He'll come. Or maybe you already know him."

"No, no. *Eish!* At my age, that time is long gone," Jess said. "Get back to the dough. You don't want it sitting for too long."

During lunch hour, Jess called Detective Meyer to inform him of her visit to the Barons and what she thought, but he wasn't amused.

"You talked to the Barons without telling me?" he asked.

"Well, I didn't see the reason not to. I'll let you know in advance next time. Tell me, have they had any issues with the police?" Jess asked.

"I've had no brushes with them. Mostly it's been to attend to incidents at their businesses. But they've never been here for anything illegal."

Jess prodded. "Did you hear anything about them not having a great sales deal with Al for the property?"

"No one says the numbers, but from what I heard, they both made a lot of money from that sale."

"What if there was someone else who wanted the property? Would they have been angry at Al and bumped him off?"

Detective Meyer grunted. "That's a new way of looking at things. But it's a little farfetched. Did they give you any names?"

"No, they just said they turned down other offers."

"Well, I don't think there's any merit to it, then."

Jess sighed. He was right. There was nothing unusual about the conversation. Precious and Prince were in the clear and there were no fresh leads to go on. Except one.

"I also went to see Luan the other day," Jess said.

The detective sighed, clearly displeased with her assertiveness. "What about?"

"Just to talk about his working relationship with Al. Don't worry, I used the fact that they still owe me cash for the service to see him. While I was there, I noticed there's a small gym in between his office and Al's. And on his table there was a bottle of homemade energy drink."

"How do you know it was a homemade energy drink?"

"He told me. Then it got me thinking: could he be using the chemical you talked about? Also, he was at the launch, and Al would've hung around him, suspecting nothing. Besides that, they were having a tussle about the business, which maybe threatened Luan's position. I think you should look into him," Jess said.

"Hmm, sounds interesting."

"It sure is. So, will you talk to him?"

"Sure. When I get back in a few days."

Jess frowned. "Get back from where?"

"I'm taking a few days off."

Jess' eyes widened in disbelief. "But what if the suspects cover up all the evidence?"

"Murder is very hard to hide. But you're not a detective, so wouldn't know," the detective replied. "Don't talk to anyone else while I'm gone. We'll take it from here. Thanks for the tip and have a great day."

The line went dead, and it left Jess staring at her phone. She didn't like his casual reaction to the information she gave him. Did he really consider Luan a suspect?

Jess knew she wouldn't wait for the detective to get back from his off days. Time was of the essence, and she now had no choice but to disobey his request to hold back.

17

Impatiently, Jess took off her apron and told Penny she was stepping out.

"Where to?" Penny asked.

"To meet a client."

Jess drove across town to the AR offices. As she drew near, she created a story for Luan: she wanted to propose an open day event where she could serve her baked treats as prospective clients explored the AR projects.

When she got to the swanky reception, she met the young receptionist again. She was wearing a beige suit this time, but her smile was less genuine, as if something was off. "Welcome back again," she said. "Are you looking to see Mr. Luan?"

"Yes I am, thanks. Is he in?"

"He's not in. He's actually not going to come in for a few days now," the receptionist replied, her smile fading.

"Is everything okay?"

"I'm not sure. What did you discuss the day you came?"

"Just a bit of business, and I passed my condolences after losing your boss," Jess replied. "Why?"

"Luan has been acting strangely since that day. He stopped taking meetings and stopped coming into work. Then he said he's taking two weeks off, without explanation."

"Has there been something else bothering him other than Al's passing?"

The receptionist sighed. "There was a big deal that he wanted to close. But how's he closing it from home?"

"You think he's working from home?" Jess asked.

"That's my guess. He still responds to emails here and there and clears office payments."

"Could you give me his home address? I'll go have a look because we haven't finished our conversation," Jess suggested.

The receptionist scribbled his address on a sticky note. "Don't tell him where you got it."

Jess smiled. "You have nothing to worry about. Thanks."

Luan lived in an upmarket apartment block called the Savannah Residences. From the outside, they looked austere, with their sandy-brown walls and darkened windows. Inside, the walls were covered in marble and everything was pristine. She took the lift to the fifth floor and walked down the carpeted corridor to Apartment 54. She rang the bell and waited. Nothing happened. She rang again, this time longer.

The din of the bell echoed lightly across the corridor. Still nothing. A door opened a few feet from her and a young woman dressed in a pilot's uniform emerged. She pulled behind her a small luggage bag on wheels. As she walked past, she stopped.

"You're here to see Luan?"

"Yes. I've been ringing for a while now."

"Oh, he went out-of-town yesterday."

Jess' eyes widened. "Out of town? To where?"

"I bumped into him at the airstrip yesterday. He said he was flying to the Mpumalanga region, but he didn't say where. Maybe you can try calling him?"

"Okay, I will. Thanks," Jess replied.

The pilot walked to the lift, and Jess was alone in the corridor again. She hadn't wanted to call him, just in case he got cold feet about meeting her. But now she had no choice. She called his number four times, and each time it went to voicemail. Luan had vanished.

Jess called Detective Meyer. "Luan might've skipped town."

"How do you know this?" the detective asked.

"I'm standing outside his apartment's door right now. He's not here and one of his neighbours has just confirmed seeing him at the airstrip yesterday."

She heard the detective groan. "I told you not to talk to anyone."

"Are you going to argue with me or chase after him?"

The detective grunted. "I'll pass the word around to the boys and our colleagues in Mpumalanga. We'll get him."

Jess felt drained, and didn't want to head back to the bakery. She drove home instead and was met by Will's excited demeanour when she walked into the house.

"Mum, I've got news for you," he said.

"Is it good or bad? Because if it's bad news, it can wait," Jess said as she slumped her large frame into her favourite couch.

"It's great news. I'm starting a delivery business."

Jess raised a brow. "You? Do deliveries?"

"Why not? I've ordered a few pizzas over the last few weeks and talked to the delivery guys, so I have a good idea how they work."

"How will you do that without a driving license?"

Will raised his left hand to show a laminated driving license.

"How long have you had that?" Jess asked.

"For a month now. I've been taking classes and practicing a lot. Now I have my car to work with."

Jess smiled. "Okay. I won't lie, I'm a little impressed that you're getting back your initiative."

"It's always been there. So, you're going to give me a delivery contract?"

Her smile disappeared. "Oh, no way. Prove yourself first. You'll have to drive that thing for two months without an accident before I can sign you off."

"But Mum, that's not really fair. You need to give me a chance," Will protested.

Jess's phone rang. It was Tau.

"Jess, I need you to come help me," his strained voice said.

Jess sat up. "What's going on?"

"They attacked me. I'm in the hospital now like a sitting duck, and I'm afraid they'll come for me again."

18

Jess cast her fatigue aside as the adrenaline took over. She grabbed her car keys and left her bewildered son in the living room as she dashed to the hospital.

Tau had said he was at the Angel Hands Hospital, which needed her to drive across the River Mesa Bridge. During the day, the bridge had flowing traffic. But close to rush hour, it often had traffic jams and today was no exception. Jess had to endure the start-and-stop crawl of traffic for half an hour before she got through. By the time she drove into the hospital, an hour had gone by.

She quickly got the directions she needed at the reception because Tau had asked them to send her through.

"There's a policeman at the door," the nurse at reception told her. Jess felt the gravity of the situation when she heard this.

She made her way to the third floor, where the private wing of the hospital was located. It often hosted the well-to-do, so she wasn't surprised that Tau was admitted there. But in what condition was he?

Sure enough, there was a uniformed policeman outside his room.

"I'm Jess. Tau asked me to come and see him," she said.

"Let me see your identification."

Jess took out her driving license.

The officer studied it. "He said he wanted to see Jess, not Jessica."

She could see him weighing his options. "Jess is short for Jessica."

Hearing this, he waved her through.

Jess opened the door to his room and heard the familiar beep of machines from inside. She hated hospitals and often avoided them.

"You came," Tau said. He lay on a large bed in a spacious room. On both sides of the bed were two seats and some machines. The curtain was drawn over the large window and the walls were immaculately clean. A flat screen TV on the wall was on, playing music videos without sound.

But the room and its distractions didn't matter to her. His form caught her attention. As she walked to him, she saw the bandage wrapped around his scalp. His left hand was also bandaged.

"Sorry to see you like this," Jess said.

Tau smiled. "I'll be okay. You should see the guy who attacked me. He's much worse."

"So it was only one guy? He's in the same hospital?"

"No, he was arrested and taken to the station first," Tau said. "And I was kidding. He hit me good and isn't as hurt as I am."

"Who attacked you?"

"Samkelo, of all people."

Jess's eyes widened. "Samkelo? How did this happen?"

"I think he followed me. I had just had coffee with a friend and was headed to my car. It was parked in the building's basement, thinking if no one saw it, then they couldn't tail it. But he had followed me there and was waiting in the shadows. He sprung at me, shouting about wanting his money back. Then we started brawling. He caught me by surprise, but I put up a fight. Fortunately, security guards came and helped me out. Then the police came, and he was arrested."

"Oh my. I'm so sorry. How bad is it?"

"I know the bandage makes it look bad, but I'm fine. They've done all the scans needed. I've only got bruises, nothing's broken. But after this, I want to get out of town. This has become a bit too much for me," Tau said.

"You don't have to do that. The police are watching over you," Jess said.

"But for how long? What if they release him on bail?"

Jess smiled at him. "For as long as it takes, regardless of whether he's released. I'll make sure of that."

She stayed with him for another half hour, easing his worries. It was already dark when she left for the police station. When she got there, she found Detective Meyer talking to Detective Mason in the lobby. Detective Mason excused herself and left, leaving Jess and Detective Meyer on their own.

"You really don't want me to take any days off, do you? You seem to know a little about every tip in the last twelve hours," Detective Meyer said.

Jess shrugged. "I call it pure coincidence. But Tau called me and told me what happened."

"I'm guessing you're here because you heard it was Samkelo," Meyer said.

"Where is he?"

"We just finished interrogating him and recording his statement."

"Did he say why he attacked Tau?"

"He says Tau's father owed him money and Tau has refused to pay him."

Jess shook his head. "Unbelievable. You know he threatened us, right?"

Detective Meyer narrowed his eyes. "When did this happen?"

"When he called Tau and tried to blackmail him."

"That's when you called me with the hypothetical question that actually wasn't hypothetical."

Jess sighed. "Yes. I didn't think it would turn out like this."

"Big mistake. I told you not to do it and you did it, anyway. Do you think you're a detective now?"

"I don't. I'm honestly just trying to help."

Detective Meyer shook his head. "But you're making things worse and now someone is hurt. One word of advice: stay in your lane. Tell me everything you think is happening before making a move. Otherwise, next time, it might be you getting hurt."

"Okay. So what happens now?"

"I have to ask him a few questions about blackmail. We can get him locked up on that and assault if you and Tau testify in court."

"We can do that. But what about Al's murder?"

Detective Meyer shook his head. "He insists he knew nothing about it."

"If he can threaten Tau and follow through, then he might have followed through on the threats he made to Al," Jess said.

"Perhaps," Detective Meyer replied. "There are police reports Al filed about it, claiming some guy called Slim John was hired to kill him. But that was years ago, and it turned out Slim John was just a smooth talker on the streets. So far, there's none linking him to the murder."

The mention of Slim John intrigued Jess. She didn't know him, but something told her she should.

"Alright. One more thing: can you please give Tau some protection? He's worried and I don't want him to skip town," Jess said.

"I already have it covered. Two officers will take turns to monitor him for a few days."

"Can it be longer?"

Detective Meyer shook his head. "I'm pretty stretched here and need all the men I can get. The sooner we solve this case, then the better for all of us."

With that, Jess left the station and headed back home. As she drove through the lighted and traffic-free streets, she mulled over the detective's words, wrestling with his warning not to do anything. But what if something came up and it would take too long for the police to get there? What then?

She found that Will had made dinner - chicken curry with rice and salad. They had just settled to eat when the doorbell rang.

"Expecting someone?" Jess asked.

Will shook his head. "No. You?"

"No."

Will walked out the door and opened it. Jess overhead a familiar voice. "Is your Mum home?"

"Mum!" Will called as Jess shot up and rushed to the door.

"Penny, what are you doing here?" Jess asked.

Penny looked tired. "I went to talk to Lawrence, and it didn't work. He's not ready to see me. I just don't feel like going back to that house right now. Can I crash with you for a few days?"

Jess smiled and grabbed Penny by the arm. "Sure. Come on in."

Penny went in and when she saw the decked out dinner table, she stopped. "Oh, sorry to interrupt."

"You're now part of our dinner table," Jess said with a smile. She caught a glance at Will's solemn reaction to Penny's appearance and made a note to talk to him about it.

After they had eaten, Jess prepped one of her daughter's bedrooms and Penny retired for the night. Jess had just said goodnight to her when Will stopped her in the corridor.

"Why are you doing this for her, Mum?"

Jess frowned. "Helping people in need is a crime now?"

"You're going out of your way for her while you can't do the same for me? All I want is a shot at starting something of my own. Why can't you support me the way you support your friends?" Will asked. With that, he went into his room and shut his door. She knocked three times, but he didn't open.

"Let's talk about this tomorrow," Jess said. As she walked to her room to turn in for the night, she felt a tinge of guilt.

19

The next morning, Jess rose early and started preparing breakfast. She was frying the omelettes when Penny walked into the kitchen.

"Good morning, Jess," Penny said. "You beat me to it."

"Good morning. Beat you to what?"

"Making breakfast."

"Well, you can prepare the tea."

Penny smiled. "I'm on it." She went to the fridge and took a packet of milk. She then filled the water kettle and started boiling water.

Over the rumbling sound of the kettle, Penny spoke. "I heard you argue with Will last night. I mean, I didn't want to, but it happened outside my door."

"Oh, that was nothing to worry about. I hope it didn't rob you of your sleep," Jess said.

"No, it didn't. But I was curious what it was about."

"It was nothing, really. The boy wants me to give him a contract to deliver our baked goods to customers, and I told him to wait a little."

"Why did you ask him to wait?"

Jess sighed as she placed the cooked omelette on a plate. "He got his driving licence a month ago and turned up the other day with that old van outside. He's hardly used to the roads, let alone driving a van. I simply told him if he can handle two months without an accident, then he's got a deal."

"Well, maybe he can do the shorter distances where there's less risk," Penny suggested.

Jess spun at her. "Are you taking his side now?"

"No. I'm just saying it's easier to keep an eye on him when he's working for you than when he's working for someone else. You can have him do a trip or two a day. It will help build his confidence."

Jess paused as the tinge of guilt returned. "You're making this hard for me."

"Well, no one said it was going to be easy," Penny replied.

"If it's going that way, then you have to chip in and keep an eye on him."

Penny smiled. "With pleasure."

"I'm making no promises, but I'll have a word with him," Jess said.

Will came down for breakfast and acted as if nothing had happened the previous night, but Jess knew she had to make amends. After they had eaten, she led him to the living room and talked to him as Penny helped with the dishes. They agreed to Penny's plan with some modifications: he'd drive four trips a day to locations that were two kilometres or less from the bakery. Will was happy with this and had a spring in his step afterwards. He went outside to check his van's condition.

Afterwards, Jess dressed up in more casual wear than usual - a pair of jeans, a t-shirt and jacket and sneakers.

Penny frowned. "Are you going for a sports event or the bakery? Because that's not you."

"I'll be passing by somewhere and this is the closest look I could think of that works." Jess said as she smoothed out her hair.

"If your plan is to look casual, then don't do that to your hair."

"I don't want to be totally casual, you know."

"You're not, but it will make you look more relaxed. Leave the hair a little ruffled."

Jess looked back at her mirror reflection. "Are you sure?"

"Trust me."

Jess put her fingers through her hair and ruffled it up slightly to a level she could live with. "That'll do it. So I'll be at the bakery around noon, in case Lerato asks."

"Where to?"

"I'll tell you when I get to work," Jess replied.

The truth was, Jess wasn't sure where she was going. She stopped by the van to check on her son. "Will, let me ask you something. Have you ever heard of a man called Slim John?"

Will stopped checking the engine and turned to her. "Slim John? How did you know that name?"

For a moment, Jess thought Will was talking as if she'd blown his identity, but she knew the man she's looking for was older.

"It's not a trick question. I really want to know."

"What's the catch?"

"There's no catch. I'm just curious."

"I don't know him personally, but I've heard of him," Will said.

"What have you heard of him?"

"He's a talented storyteller who seemed to live a crazy criminal life in the past. Why?"

"I'm curious. Do you think you can find out where he hangs out?"

Will took out his phone and stepped away. "Excuse me, let me make a call."

He spoke on the phone for close to five minutes before he returned. "He's usually on Fitz Street at the corner where the Burgerland store once was. I hope you're not going there. It's not a friendly neighbourhood."

Jess smiled. "Me? Go there? I was just curious."

She got into her car, and, of course, drove off towards Fitz Street. It was right on the edge of the only township in town, and was considered unsafe to most people. But Jess was going anyway, hoping nothing happened.

When she got to the corner, she parked her car across the street from the closed Burgerland store. There was no one on the street corner. She waited. She saw all kinds of people hit hard by life: addicts, petty thieves, hawkers, and idlers as they walked around. Some of them studied her car, but none had made a move to break in - yet. She hoped she wouldn't have to be there for hours, because eventually she might get approached and have to drive off fast.

Then a middle-aged man in an oversized jeans jacket and trousers, wearing a red beanie and matching shoes, walked up to the corner with two younger men. He was carrying a gunny sack while the two men behind him carried a wooden bench. They placed it against the wall next to the store entrance. In minutes, they had set up a board game and started playing. As they played, they chatted animatedly. But it was obvious the man in the beanie talked the most. During a brief exchange, the man in the beanie turned his back to Jess, and she read a huge embroidered label on his back: *Slim John*. For someone who was a former criminal or assassin, Jess was surprised that he didn't make it a secret who he was. What if a relative of one of his victims sought revenge? He literally had a target on his back.

She watched them play for ten more minutes, and she figured this was something they did all day. Other people came, stopped briefly to watch them, and left.

Jess pondered what to do. She assumed he had a gun, or his friends had one. Should she call him from the car? What if he mistook her for an enemy? She shelved the idea. How about driving up to where they were? Again, she figured they'd think it was an enemy. Ultimately, Jess gathered the courage to step out of the car. She considered walking up to him as a friendlier option.

She scanned around her to make sure no one was around to follow her before she got to him.

She inhaled and then opened the door. A second later, she heard someone rushing towards her from the back of the car. She swiftly shut the door, locked it and screamed in fright. A ragged man with a massive afro, one idler she'd seen earlier, stared back at her. His eyes were glazed red, and he smiled sheepishly. He didn't linger for long, for someone else shouted at him.

"Hey, get off that car!" Slim John ordered the idler, who scampered away.

A shaken Jess watched as Slim John sauntered towards her car. He soon stood next to her window and locked eyes with her.

"What are you doing here?" he asked in a playful tone.

Jess froze. Should she open the window?

"I just helped you. Are you having car trouble?" his voice getting stern. "Or are you the police?"

Jess' heart was racing. She fumbled for the car keys, but her fingers felt slippery.

"I'll count to three. You better roll down these windows or I'm getting in by force. One... Two... Three..."

Jess turned just in time to see his right arm lift something in the air. A baton. It lingered at the peak of the swing, and then it rushed fast towards her driver's window. She shut her eyes and waited for the impact.

20

Bang!

The baton struck the window, but the sound surprised Jess. It wasn't as loud or violent as she expected. She opened her eyes and saw Slim John laughing. He swung the baton in the air and then she noticed it wobble. It wasn't made of wood.

She lowered the driver's window. "What are you trying to do?"

"You scare easy. Look at this." He swung the baton some more, watching it wiggle in the air. "It's rubber. All rubber. It can hurt you if needed. You look like you're in the wrong neighbourhood."

Jess inhaled, composing herself. "I'm in the right one. I'm looking for Slim John."

"Well, you've found him. What do you want?"

"To talk to you about the Barons."

Slim John rubbed the back of his head. "Those two rich kids? Why do you want to know?"

"I hear someone once hired you to kill their father," Jess said. She wanted to tease out the storyteller in him.

"*Hayibo.* You've brought these old stories back to life? You're wondering if I finally killed him. Are you a reporter?"

"Yes, I am," Jess said, choosing to play along. "Freelance though. I'm researching on the story and it seems you know a lot about what happens in the assassin's world."

She saw his eyes sparkle. He saw a chance to get more minutes of fame, and she was going to use it to her advantage.

"First, I didn't kill him. I'm retired. Second, which magazine?"

"Street Report. It's pretty new," Jess said. "Are you going to talk to me, or should I go write my story without your input?"

He scanned the street. "We can talk. But not here. The streets have ears, you know. Also, if your car stays here for another few minutes, you'll find it with no wheels."

Slim John turned to his two friends, shouted something at them in slang she didn't understand. He then swung round to the passenger side and got in. "Let's go to my place."

"Where's that?"

He pointed out the windscreen. "See that junction? Turn left and the first house is mine. We can park your car in the compound so that no one will touch it."

Jess was half unsure about this, but took the plunge. She had come this far, anyway. She drove down the street and turned right. There was a bungalow with an open gate. Inside, there was enough room for just one more car next to the rusty wreck of a BMW E30.

Jess eased her car into the space and parked. Slim John jumped out and closed the gate. When she got out, Slim John stared at her. She towered over him.

"I thought the car was small, but clearly you are taller than I thought," he said.

"Is that a problem?"

"Nah, I got sturdy seats. If you came here three years ago, I would've even taken you for a ride in my *gusheshe*," he said, pointing at the BMW. "Perfect suspension. She used to rule the streets around here."

"You drift?" she asked, studying the car. It had modified wheel flares and a larger than normal rear wing. The body paint was a stock, cream colour.

"Yeah, but these days I have to borrow other machines. I killed my engine and I don't have the dough or patience to get another. Come into the house."

Inside his house was a mish-mash of anything he could find. Cartons, mismatched seats, three different carpets of different ages, a dusty coffee table, and blacked-out windows. Two Flat screen TVs, one on the floor with a cracked screen and another propped up on a chair, were in the living room. He had pictures of guns on the walls, which were obvious reprints from internet images. Some were decent, others were dog-eared, while a few were pixelated eyesores. It felt like she was in the house of an overgrown teen rather than that of a middle-aged man.

"It's a bit of a mess, but it works. Sit here," he said as he removed a stack of motoring magazines from one of the single seaters. It was well-worn from years of use, but as he'd promised, it could handle her large frame.

"Will you have anything? A boerewors, a bobitie? Some juice?"

"No thanks," Jess said. She knew they must be leftovers. There was no way he was going to barbecue meat into a boerewors, or bake a casserole dish like a bobotie in a rush. She wanted to spend as little time there as possible. "Let's focus on the Barons."

"They are a strange, rich, but pretty simple family. Their father was a genius investor and when he died, things changed forever for them."

"Was their house haunted?"

Slim John chuckled. "Only the simple-minded believe that. People come up with crazy theories to make sense of things."

"How about Al Rocki? What was your relationship with him?"

"None. I never knew the guy."

"Until Samkelo hired you to kill him," Jess chimed in.

Slim John scratched his chin. "That's what the police said."

"You're trying to say that you're not an assassin?"

"I was, but not for Samkelo. He couldn't afford me."

"Couldn't or wouldn't?" she prodded.

"Couldn't. We met and talked about it. I turned him down. I don't do missions for pennies."

"Let's imagine it then. If he could afford you, what would you have used?"

Slim John pursed his lips. "I know what you're trying to do, and I'm not playing that game. I'm retired, and that's all there is to it."

Jess grinned. She really wanted to believe he could do it, but from her first impressions, he had never been an assassin.

"Why haven't you asked me about the private investigator?" he posed.

Jess raised a brow. "What private investigator?"

"The one the Baron kids hired to follow Al."

Jess almost jumped from her seat. "They what? When was this?"

"As they were negotiating the deal."

She frowned. "Who's this investigator? And why did they hire him?"

Slim John stood. "Wait here."

He left. Jess sat there for close to five minutes, waiting and wondering. She braced herself, just in case Slim John had an unpleasant surprise for her.

Moments later, Slim John emerged. But he had changed his look. He now wore a pinstripe shirt, a pair of cotton trousers held up by a pair of worn suspenders, and a hat. He looked more polished than she'd expected, although the suspenders were an unnecessary accessory.

"What's going on?" Jess asked.

"I'm Johnny Slim, P.I., at your service," he replied.

Jess was about to burst out laughing when the realisation came to her. "You were the detective they hired?"

He beamed. "The one and only."

Jess shook her head in disbelief. "How did you pull it off?"

"I've read a lot of books and I have a degree in theatre arts. I love a performance."

Jess wasn't sure if he was putting on a performance right now, but it intrigued her. "But you didn't do the course work for a license to practise."

He pointed to a corner of the living room, and Jess saw the framed licence hanging there. She stood and walked to it. She studied it carefully, although she'd never seen one before. This meant she didn't know if it was legitimate, but it looked convincing.

"Why would you do this?" she asked.

"A man has to eat," he replied.

After taking another minute running scenarios in her mind, Jess asked: "Tell me something - why did they hire you to follow Al? And I mean the real reason."

"I already gave you the reason they told me. For the absolute truth, you'll have to talk to Precious herself."

"It was her idea to hire you?"

He nodded. "She led every single meeting we had. Her brother tagged along reluctantly. He wanted to fast track the whole deal, but she wanted to dot her i's and cross her t's."

"How long did she have you on payroll? And what was she keen on the most?"

"I worked for her until two weeks before Al launched the motel. She mainly wanted to know his routine. Where he ate. Who he met. His mannerisms."

Jess' eyes narrowed. "What do you think she knows about his death?"

He shrugged. "You'll have to ask her. I can't say anymore."

"Why not?"

He sighed. "I may have been a killer once, but every hunter soon becomes the hunted. I'm not interested in running."

21

Jess stood up to leave. "Fair enough. I'll talk to my editor and then we can plan a proper interview and photo-shoot."

Slim John beamed. "Pictures, eh? So I should prepare my clothes. I've got plenty that I've not used."

"Can I have your number?"

"Of course, of course," Slim John said as he handed her a business card. It had a phone number and *John Slim, Private Investigator,* printed on it.

Jess got into her car as Slim John opened the gate. She backed out and drove off fast. As she went past the former Burgerland, she saw a crowd of onlookers had formed around the bench as a heated game ensued. She was sure Slim John was going to change back to his street wear and join them. He seemed to her to be a chameleon, a man who understood his environment so well that he went the extra mile to blend in.

Her mind drifted back to the Baron siblings. It seemed Precious had much more to tell than she previously thought. Maybe it was time to make use of her offer for a direct call.

When she got to the bakery, Jess saw Will's old van parked on the side street next to the building. She went up to the van and found him slouched inside, playing a game on his phone.

"*Eish*. You can't be serious," she said.

Startled, Will almost dropped his phone. "Mum, you had me going for a minute."

"As it should be. What are you doing out here?"

"Waiting for my first delivery," Will said with a smile.

Jess shook her head. "I'm not sure there's one lined up just yet."

"Penny said she'd make it happen."

Of course, Penny would, Jess mused. A thought crossed her mind. "You have data bundles on your phone, right?"

"Yeah. Why?"

"Here's some legal work for you: look up any court mentions about the sale of the House of Baron. Let me know what comes up. That might make your delivery assignment speed up," Jess said with a wink.

Will grinned. "I'm on it."

Jess went into the bakery and found Penny and Lerato hard at work, churning out gingerbread cookies by the dozen.

"We got an order for a kids' party tomorrow," Lerato said as she gave Jess the once over. "Since when do you wear all jeans? Are you from a 90s-themed concert or something?"

145

"Don't let Penny influence your view of me," Jess said.

Penny raised her hands. "I had nothing to do with it."

"Can we talk for a sec?" Jess asked Penny.

"Sure," Penny said as she walked over. They spoke in low tones.

"So I just got back from the place I didn't tell you about. I have a sneaky feeling the Barons had something to do with Al's death," Jess whispered.

Penny's eyes widened. "Both of them?"

"I'm not sure. But a little bird told me to talk to Precious about it. How do I approach her?"

"Well, you could offer to sell her cookies," Penny suggested.

Jess shook her head. "I already introduced myself as a lawyer."

"Why would you do that?"

"I was making things up as I went along. I was once an intern lawyer, and it often comes up as a backup persona when needed."

Penny pursed her lips while tapping her index finger on the counter. "You know what? Just go along with that. I don't know what a lawyer would say, though."

Just then, the door jingled. It was Will entering the store. He walked over to them. "Mum, I've found something."

"What?" Jess asked.

"Over a year ago, the Barons took a case to court stating that the sale they made to Al was irregular. They wanted Al to give back the property. But the court dismissed the case," Will said.

"Talk about lightning striking twice. And that is what I'll use to get Precious to talk to me," Jess said, as she took out her phone with a grin.

Sure enough, Precious was willing to see her. Jess convinced Penny to take her, but only after Lerato consented. When they arrived and parked outside the large Baron home, they were told the siblings were working the farm. The housekeeper directed them down a dirt road that led there. She advised them to drive as it was over a kilometre away.

Jess drove down the dirt road, which ended abruptly, and they were soon on bumpy grassland as they inched closer to the farm. They could see two John Deere tractors tilling the land in opposite directions. Jess drove until her small hatchback got close to a low, man-made ridge that her car couldn't go over. She stopped the car, and they both got out.

"Can you make out which of them is in which tractor?" Penny asked.

Jess put her right palm over her eyes like a visor to block the afternoon sun. "I think she's in the older one that's closest to us."

She waved to Precious' tractor and saw the cap-wearing Precious wave back in her cab. Precious drove the tractor closer to them. She stopped and came down the machine.

"Welcome to farm life," Precious said, smiling while taking off her cap and wiping her brow. "You came with your assistant?"

Jess nodded. "Yes, she's Penny. It looks like hard work."

"People have no idea how hectic it is to run a farm."

"I always wanted to run one, but now you're giving me the impression I'm not ready," Jess said. "I came across an article online that you went to court to contest the sale of the House of Baron to Al. What was that about?"

"We just wanted Al to do the right thing. We thought the valuation was a little off, but the court thought otherwise."

"Why did you think the valuation was off? You had your own property valuer, right?"

"We did, but we later found out he was a friend to Al. So we had to look into that conflict of interest and found out he may have underquoted," Precious said.

Jess frowned. "How did you find out the connection?"

"We had someone look into it."

"Is this the private investigator you hired?" Jess prodded.

Precious' face darkened. "Private investigator?"

"Yes, you hired one to follow Al, right?"

Precious turned to leave. "I've got nothing to say to you."

"Was he the one that told you about the valuer?"

By this time, Precious had reached the tractor and was going on board again. She shut the door, revved its engine, and it chugged out of the dirt.

"Why won't you talk about it?" Jess shouted.

The tractor, which was five feet away, suddenly spun in their direction and Precious gunned the engine. It was coming straight at them, and something rooted Jess to the spot, like a deer in the headlights.

22

A yank to her right arm helped Jess snap out of her shock.

"*Yhoo*, let's move!" Penny shouted as she dragged Jess away from the tractor's path.

Jess came to her senses and gave in to Penny's strong pull backwards, nearly falling over. She regained her balance, and they hurried over the low ridge and towards the car.

They could hear the roaring tractor bearing down on them, and then it started groaning. Jess stopped by her car and, as she opened the driver's door, she turned to see the tractor heaving and puffing. It was struggling to make it up the ridge. She heard a loud cranking sound as Precious struggled with the gear lever.

"Something's wrong with the transmission," Jess muttered.

"Then let's get out of here before she sorts it out," Penny said as she jumped into the car.

Jess got into the driver's seat and was about to start the car when she saw Precious jump out of the tractor and run towards the warehouse.

"She's running," Jess exclaimed as she got out to run. She felt her lungs lament as she struggled to run faster. It wasn't her cup of tea, especially with her enormous frame. She vowed she'd hit the gym again once it was all over. However, Penny had no such problem. Being younger and smaller, she soon overtook her and closed in on the target. Just as Precious was getting close to the warehouse door, Penny tackled her.

They tussled in the gravel dirt, rolling this way and that while shrieking. There was pulling of hair and tearing of clothes, and attempts at punches and slaps. Jess closed in and used her frame and strength to subdue Precious. Penny grabbed some worn out sisal rope placed near the warehouse door to tie Precious' arms behind her. They sat her down with her back against the warehouse walls.

"Why were you running?" Jess asked as her heaving chest gasped for breath.

Precious didn't answer as she too composed her breathing.

"You know something about Al's death, don't you?"

Precious shot her a look. "He didn't deserve that property. That was our home, our legacy!"

"What did you do, Precious?" Jess asked.

"I did what I had to do. He and his son had it coming, the way they treated us like dirt. I wish I got to the son too. He caught a lucky break."

Jess raised a brow. "You're talking about Tau?"

"Who do you think I'm talking about?"

"Pree!" a distant voice shouted.

Jess turned to see Prince standing next to Precious' tractor. He spotted them and they locked eyes. Prince ran towards them, wielding a pitchfork in his hands. He held it aloft and pointed its tines towards them.

Penny waved at him and pointed at his sister, telling him with gestures that she was their hostage. Prince slowed down and lowered the pitchfork, but his eyes were still raging.

"What's going on here?" Prince asked.

"It's about Al," Jess said.

"What about him?"

Precious broke down in tears.

Prince squatted to her level. "Pree..?"

Precious blurted out. "A lot is going to happen from this moment onwards. A lot of things that you never imagined. You'll have to take care of this place. And when you think about me, remember this: I did it for us. I did it for Dad."

23

Jess studied Prince's reaction.

His jaw was wide open. "What are you talking about? What did you do?"

Precious pursed her lips. "I got justice for us. I got justice for Dad."

Then it dawned on Prince, and he stood up. "No, no, no..." He turned around and placed both hands atop his head in exasperation.

"You're telling me you did this on your own?" Jess asked.

"He had nothing to do with it," Precious said.

"How did you do it?" Jess asked.

Sirens started sounding in the distance. Everyone looked up, as if expecting a police car to fall from the sky.

"Is that..." Precious began before her voice trailed off.

"Yes, it's the police. I called them while heading here," Jess said. "How did you do it?"

Precious shook her head. "I want my lawyer."

Jess sighed. She could do nothing except wait.

Prince didn't put up a fight as he watched his sister get arrested by the police. He was devastated, and Jess felt sorry for him.

A few days later, Jess was at the bakery when Detective Meyer stopped by.

"What will you be having?" Jess asked.

"Two doughnuts to go, please," Detective Meyer said. "Plus a quick chat outside."

Once she'd served him, they went outside and stood in the shade of a jacaranda tree that was popping its first purple flowers.

"I wanted to talk to you about the case, and what the progress is so far," Detective Meyer said. "I'm only doing this because you helped us get some arrests done, and for that, I'm grateful. However, I'm also not happy that you got some people hurt."

"I'm sorry about it, you know that," Jess said.

"Sometimes staying out of the way is better, especially if you're untrained, which you are. Leave the tough assignments to us, okay?"

Jess sighed and nodded. "Okay."

"Good. So, about Precious, she bought the drugs at one of those downtown chemists that have both counterfeit and illegal drugs. You can find anything there. But the dose she got was of a higher concentration than what the government approves. She met Al the night before the launch and spiked his homemade energy drink. I think it's the same energy drink Al and Luan used to make and use when they worked out together."

"Wait. Who told you about that?"

"Luan resurfaced after the arrests. He felt the heat was on him and went incognito. When he returned, he first came down to the station to state his case. He was already in the clear, so there was no need for it, but I could understand his anxiety. We let him go to get his life back on track."

Jess tilted her head right. "Oh, I see. How did she spike his drink?"

"Time and chance. She waited for Al to get distracted and spiked his drink bottle, which was on his table. I think he already prepped his drink or did so the next morning. Whichever way, the poison was inside when he drank it. It seems when he went to take his other medication, he drank the energy drink to ease the swallow. Fatal mistake. We got the bottle again and tested it. We found traces of the chemical, so the confession adds up. No one else talked about the bottle except her."

"Do you think she gave him an overdose?"

"Most likely, especially since she was doing it in a hurry," Detective Meyer replied. "It ended up in a heart attack and Al was gone."

Jess wiped her brow. "How about her motive? She said she did it for Prince and her father."

Detective Meyer nodded. "She claimed she didn't want to lose all the property their father left them, especially his favourite. Prince pushed the sale through since he's more business-minded than she is, although it's hard to explain all the properties that have collapsed on their watch. I think Precious panicked that they'd run out of revenue sources. When she read Al's plans for the motel, she wanted to hijack the process and rebuild it herself."

"Makes sense. How about Prince?"

"He wasn't involved."

Jess was about to ask about Slim John and remembered she hadn't told the detective about him. It didn't matter anymore, anyway. The case was going to trial and Precious would be locked up for many years to come.

The detective bit into his doughnut and walked to his car. "Stay out of trouble and keep your nose out of affairs the police should deal with. You hear?"

"I hear you," Jess said. She watched the police car drive away and stood on the sidewalk for a few more minutes. She stared up and saw the purple flowers blooming in the soft caress of the sun and felt a peace wash over her. It was over.

A week later, she attended Al's funeral. Tau had recovered and was moving around easily with a few bruises. After they had buried him at the family cemetery, Tau walked up to Jess and hugged her.

"Thanks for everything," Tau said.

"You're welcome, son."

He ended the embrace. "I've decided to sell a stake of the motel to Prince, in honour of both our dead fathers. Since we grieve together, we can also thrive together."

"Are you sure?" Jess asked.

Ava Zuma

"I've never been more certain in my life. Besides, he has a better ear for business than I do."

Jess smiled. It sounded like a great idea. She hoped they'd be able to bury any hatchet they shared.

In all-black outfits, Jess, Penny, and Lerato headed back to the car.

"I think we should take the day off," Lerato suggested.

Penny's eyes enlarged. "Since when have you been a fan of time off?"

"Since today. Life's too short, and we all need to enjoy it," Lerato replied. "How are things with your hubby?"

Penny and Jess exchange looks. The previous night, they'd invited her husband Lawrence for a chat. Jess had done her best to convince both of them to understand each other first. This went on till late in the night. The outcome was promising.

"We made amends, and moved back together, thanks to Jess," Penny gushed. "We're even planning a getaway holiday together."

"I suspect it's a one-way ticket to anywhere exotic," Jess remarked.

They laughed.

"You guys can head home to your husbands. I'll spend some time at the bakery with my junior husband."

Lerato's forehead furrowed. "Junior what?"

"My son. He's coming over to do some deliveries."

"You finally came round?" Penny asked with a gentle nudge.

"We're going to go for our first drive, so there are no guarantees," Jess said.

Indeed, there were none. When she got back to the bakery, she loaded two cartons of cupcakes and then got into the passenger seat of the van. The seats, though old, were comfortable.

"Let's head out to Oceania," Jess said, an estate that was a kilometre and a half away.

"You're coming?" Will asked. "It's not that far."

"The better," Jess said with a chuckle. "The less time I spend on this, the better."

The van came to life and chugged along at slow speeds through the streets. It was too loud, but seemed to drive well, Jess thought. They had hardly gone past the kilometre mark when something started rattling underneath the car.

"What's that?" an alarmed Jess asked.

Will slowed down and pulled over to the side of the road. "I don't know."

He jumped off the car and scanned the bottom of the van. He rose and sighed.

"The exhaust fell off its mount at the back. I need a wire to tie it back until we get to a mechanic."

Jess shook her head. "Old things break all the time."

"It's not really broken if I can find the wire I'm looking for."

They both laughed and searched the car. They were in a section of highway that had speeding cars, and their lifted thumbs couldn't convince someone to stop.

Will started getting discouraged. But the calm manner in which he was handling it impressed Jess. No frantic calls, no raised voices. Just taking it easy, one step at a time.

Then it hit her: she had several barrettes, her metal hair clips. "'Can hair clips work?"

Will stopped and turned to her. "Yes, let's try them."

They spent the next half hour joining the different clips together and improvising an exhaust hold.

When she got back into the van, Jess felt fuzzy. It was a good thing to fix things with your son. She felt she and her son had the confidence to figure it out, whatever the situation. This, alongside solving Al's murder, had given her supreme confidence.

Maybe she had a thing for solving puzzles. But a murder case was a one-in-a-million situation. She didn't need to expect any more mysterious deaths, right?

The End

Afterword

Thank you for reading Cookies and Haunted Screams. I really hope you enjoyed reading it as much as I had writing it!

If you have a minute, please consider leaving a review on Amazon or the retailer where you got it.

Many thanks in advance for your support!

The Sweet Smell Of Disaster

Chapter 1 Sneak Peek

It was a sunny morning and Jessica Nomvete, or Jess as her friends called her, was buzzing as she strolled down the street towards her bakery. There were a few people on the street in the small country town. A gentle breeze blew on her face and orange sun's rays kissed the single story rooftops of the buildings on the main street.

The beautiful thing about living in the small town of Fort Bay was the weather. It was never too hot nor too cold, and while the sun shone for a good part of the year, rain was equally a blessing to experience. Winters were cool and featured no frost, which was perfect for the various grape farms that covered the landscape and made the place one of the highest producers of South African wine.

Jess had parked two blocks away at a newly opened parking bay after the town council started road works on the parking spot outside the bakery, but she didn't mind. She moved her six feet tall, wholesome frame with a surprising agility that belied the fact that she was in her mid-fifties. She wore a pleated dress and carried a handbag over her left shoulder. But she wanted to get out of them soon, for in her right hand was a garment bag containing two new dresses.

It was some minutes to nine when she arrived at Yummy Bites Bakery, and found, alongside the inviting scent of baked goods, her two colleagues already setting up for the day. The small speakers suspended near the ceiling played soft tones of South African house music, which was apt for the beginning of the day. It always puts you in a good mood.

"*Sawubona,* my friends! How's the morning?" Jess said as she sauntered to the counter.

Lerato Ndaba, her friend and business partner, eyed her over the thick-rimmed glasses she wore. "Good morning to you, too."

The younger lady, Penny Mtanse, smiled. "You're glowing today."

"*Eish,* I'd better be. There's something I need to show you now, now," Jess said as she made a beeline for the wash-rooms, next to the back office.

"What is it?" Lerato asked.

"Just wait, you'll see," Jess replied. She decided the washroom was too small to change comfortably and went into the back office. It was a small square office that had enough room to fit a working desk, three chairs, and a file cabinet. It also had a full-length mirror on one wall, which was ideal. Jess unzipped the garment bag and took out the two dresses. One was a silk emerald coloured dress, while the other was a colourful, flowing Ndebele-patterned dress. She preferred the emerald dress. Although it was figure hugging and she no longer had the wasp waist anymore, she felt she had a few curves she could flaunt. However, the flowing dress had its traditional flair and colours that drew you in. She had to choose one, which was a dilemma, and hoped her colleagues would help her decide.

She wore the emerald dress first, checked herself in the mirror, took a deep breath, and stepped out. As she did her best cat walking impression to the front, Jess hoped no customer had walked in. Fortunately, it was unlikely at that hour. As soon as the two women saw her, their eyes widened.

Penny's jaw dropped. "Oh wow, that's so lovely. I've never seen you wear one of those."

This was true. Jess liked nothing fancy. Life was made to be simple. But today was different. "Why, thank you. It's good to see you appreciate it. I love it."

"It looks amazing on you," Penny continued.

Lerato grunted. "The dress is nice, I agree. But where's the other one?"

Jess frowned. "You'll see it. Why don't you give your remarks on this one first?"

"I have. It's a nice dress. Can we see the other one?" Lerato said.

"Lerato, come on. We all know it's a nice dress. How does it look on me, though?" Jess asked.

"I'll tell you after I see the other one," Lerato insisted.

That was all Jess needed to hear. She'd known Lerato almost all her life, and knew that she wasn't impressed.

"This is my favourite," Jess said so that they knew where she stood. She made her way to the back office. Ten minutes later, she returned wearing the Ndebele-patterned dress.

A collective whistle filled the room.

Penny clapped. "That's majestic."

"What are the dresses for?" Lerato asked, cupping her face in her hands.

"Lerato, why aren't you just saying how they look first?" Jess asked.

"I want to know where you want to use them so that I can tell you what fits."

Jess shook her head and turned to Penny. "Give me more feedback. You like it?"

Penny nodded fast, her long, natural hair waving in the air. "I love it, I love it. Even more than the other one."

"You're sure?" Jess asked.

"Do a twirl, and I'll tell you." Jess did a twirl, and by the time she came to rest, Penny was smiling from ear to ear. "Yeah, that's the one. I'm sure now."

Lerato grinned. "You know what? That's the dress that will win hearts over. But why did you want our votes?"

"I'm going to wear one of them soon," Jess replied.

"To where?"

"It's a surprise."

Lerato sighed. "Come on, spill the beans. There's nothing new under the sun."

Jess smiled. "True. I've been invited to attend the Governor's Ball."

The two ladies gasped.

"You're now swimming with the high and mighty," Lerato said.

"I've always wanted to go to the Ball. They look so fancy there," Penny remarked.

Jess shook her head. "Frankly, it's not my cup of tea. But it's never too late to try something new, right?"

"How did you get in?" Penny asked.

Jess winked. "It's good to know people. They might surprise you with great news."

"Speaking of great news, we have some too," Jess interjected.

Jess raised a brow. "Really?"

"Yeah," Lerato replied. "We're planning to enter the Rowe Annual Baking Competition."

Jess let out a heavy sigh. "Guys…"

"No, no, no. Before you say it, Let me just say I believe we can win it this year," Lerato added.

"I agree," Penny said.

Jess shook her head. "We've been runners up three years in a row. Three years!"

"We just have to give them something they've never seen before. This is the year," Lerato said.

Jess crossed her arms. "Oh? And what will you offer them this year that we haven't tried? The audience voted for our cakes and treats as the best of the class last year, but the judges always vote the other way."

"We lost by one vote," Lerato replied.

"One vote is a lot."

"This year we get to cross that line."

"Well, I wish you luck," Jess said as she turned to go to the back office.

"Wait a minute. You're going to be with us, right?" Penny asked.

Jess shook her head. "The competition is fourteen days away. You need more prep time than that to win it. I'm not doing it."

"Don't do this, Jess. We're a team," Lerato urged.

"You'll have to do it without me. But I'm with you in spirit," Jess replied.

"Are you seriously choosing the Ball over us?" Lerato asked. "Or is this about Helena?"

Jess grinned. "You know, it's about time I met her."

"Traitor," Lerato said with a teasing smile.

"Call me whatever you want. But Helena is the perfect idea of grace under fire. That woman is always smart, poised, gracious, and has the aura of excellence I just can't put a finger on until I meet her."

Penny put a hand up. "Hold on. Those dresses are kind of Helena's style."

Jess smiled. "She's worn something similar. But you know she does designer wear, so I have to talk to my tailor nicely to get something close and affordable. But judging from your reactions, he hit the bull's eye. What better way to say she inspires me?"

"I couldn't agree more," Penny said.

Lerato grunted. "Well, I don't agree with choosing that over us. We'll still enter the competition. The door is open if you want to join us."

"No, thanks. I'll..." Jess began, but was interrupted as the door jingle sounded.

A young woman in a smart dress suit and high heels walked in. She had a natural beauty that needed no makeup, although she'd applied some lip gloss. Her smile was warm.

"Hello, Jess," the new arrival said.

"Stacy. What on earth are you doing here?" Jess asked as she walked over to her. They embraced.

"I came to see you about something. You look dashing in that."

"Thanks. If you see it again at the ball, act surprised, okay? L et me introduce you," Jess said, turning to her colleagues. "Ladies, this is Stacy. She's a good friend I met at one event we served at two years ago. She's also the personal assistant of the Governor's wife, so you can guess where the invitation came from."

"Nice to meet you," Penny and Lerato said in near unison.

"Can we talk outside?" Stacy asked.

"No way. Let's go to the back office. I'm not ready to be seen in public dressed like this," Jess said as she led her to the back office.

They entered the office and shut the door.

"Pardon the mess. What's up?" Jess asked.

"It's about the event."

"I hope it's not bad news."

Stacy pursed her lips. "It depends on how you'll take it."

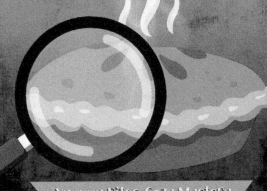

THE
Sweet
SMELL OF
DISASTER

Yummy Bites Cozy Mystery

AVA ZUMA

Also By Ava Zuma

Yummy Bites Cozy Mystery Series

Cookies and Haunted Screams (Book 1)

The Sweet Smell of Disaster (Book 2)

A Recipe for Catastrophe – **COMING SOON**

A Sprinkling of Murder – **COMING SOON**

Yummy Bites, Deadly Frights – **COMING SOON**

The Sunshine Cove Cozy Mystery Series

Makeup and Mayhem (Book 1)

Eyebrows and Evil Looks (Book 2)

Nails and Nightmare (Book 3)

Highlighters and Upheaval (Book 4)

Christmas Carols and Lipstick Perils (Book 5)

Foundation and Temptations (Book 6)

The Westbay City Mystery Series

End of the Road (Book 1)

Road to Disaster (Book 2)

Bump in the Road (Book 3)

Newsletter Signup

Want **FREE** COPIES OF FUTURE **CLEANTALES** BOOKS, FIRST
NOTIFICATION OF NEW RELEASES, CONTESTS AND
GIVEAWAYS?

GO TO THE LINK BELOW TO SIGN UP TO THE
NEWSLETTER!

https://cleantales.com/newsletter/

38300290R00106